What's the Deal with Joshua Reynolds?

Tales from Huntsville, Volume 2

L.R. Watkins

Published by L.R. Watkins, 2024.

Also by L.R. Watkins

Tales from Huntsville
What Ever Happened to Ellyn Lyss?
What's the Deal with Joshua Reynolds?

Table of Contents

To my grandmother, who always believed in me even
when I didn't.

Introduction

Joshua braced himself for what he assumed would be the end of his life. His dad prepared to launch his fist into Joshua's face.

When the crushing blow came, he was surprised he hadn't lost consciousness. He resumed his pleading.

"Please, Dad, please, just give me another chance." he begged.

His father looked down on him with a grimace of hate. "No," he said. "No more chances. I told you what I wanted you to get for me, and you failed. Again. Now get out of my house before I have your brother escort you out for me."

Stifling a sob, Joshua rose resolutely to his feet. A sense of courage overcame him. *If I have to leave, I'm going to do it my way,* he thought to himself.

Aloud, he told his father: "Dad, I'm sick of you always harping on me to steal stuff for you. You're perfectly capable of doing in yourself, you just make me do it because you don't want to get caught."

As his father's outraged look, Joshua mustered up his strength and continued. "I'm fifteen, Dad, and this is 1975. I may be leaving because you demand it, but I'm not looking back."

His father muffled an outburst of rage, and Joshua felt a sense of satisfaction. He wasn't sure if his words had hit the mark, but somehow the look on his father's face told him they had.

Quietly, with Joshua's back to the door, eyes on his father, he slowly walked to the front door. "See you, Dad," he said simply. "Tell my brother I'll miss him."

And just like that, Joshua stepped into a whole different world. Without looking back.

"A few days and you'll be back to normal." AJ told Joshua approvingly. "My, my. Reynolds, aren't you a one, eh? Going back to defeat the Champion tonight?"

Joshua Reynolds shook his head. "No, AJ, I'm sunk. I haven't won a fair fight in an age, it feels like. No, the wrestling life don't seem like it's for me."

AJ put on a disapproving frown. "Kid, you have it all, the physique, the smile, all of it. Why are you throwing it away?"

Joshua stifled a sigh. "My dad kicked me out three weeks ago, AJ. I knew I could turn to you, or else I wouldn't have survived this long. I appreciate all you've done for me, but honestly, I can't keep getting beaten up like this. How would you like to go around with a black eye?" Joshua shook his head. "Sometimes I think I should just go back to my dad and ask for forgiveness, or something. Anything is better than living on the streets."

AJ looked taken aback. "Now, you can't mean that, can you, Josh? I mean, look at you, you're a little beat up, sure, but nothing a little experience can't teach you. Tell you what, you stay on with me for another week, and I'll see what we can do to make your life even better."

Joshua growled in frustration. "No! Enough of this. I quit." He stalked away, into the night.

As Joshua walked down the dark alley, he reflected on all his life had been, all that it still could be. As AJ had said, he did have a lot of potential, so why waste it?

He wouldn't waste it; but he wouldn't spend it fighting in wrestling rings either. No, there must be something else he could do. Something...

As Joshua returned to his memories, a feeling of fear crossed him. When he quit school several months ago, he had no idea what others thought of him. But now... What could his teachers be saying about him? What of his old chums and buddies? He needed some help, that was for sure. There must be someone who would take him in, surely. But who?

Joshua inwardly chided himself. No, he was going about this all wrong. He simply needed to forget the past memories and go on to the future. But when had the future ever looked this dim? Unfortunately, the past was even dimmer.

Because it was the past he was running from, the past he was attempting to escape. It was the past that kept him awake at night, staring at the ceiling for hours at end.

If only he could change the past, then everything would be different. For one, he wouldn't be out on the streets, looking for a job, or who knew what.

Certainly, there must be something he could do. But with a belabored sigh, he realized there was nothing, nothing he could possibly do to change his circumstances. He crumbled into a bewildered heap on the pavement. The memories swirled in around him, crushing him with their vibrant power.

And he felt himself being swept away...

Chapter 1

1968 When Joshua was born, there was no joy. Now, eight years later, that same little boy had little of the joy so many of his playmates claimed.

He was a downcast child, only speaking when spoken to, or yelled at. His voice was always heard barely above a whisper, when he spoke at all, which was hardly ever.

Despite his lack of speech, Joshua had many friends. Whether it was because of his good looks at such a young age, or his gentle personality, no one could tell for sure. But little boys and girls flocked around him, doting on him. He probably received more attention from his friends than he ever received from his father.

His father hated him, of that, he was certain. Joshua's mother had died while birthing him, due to a sickness that had left her weak and thin. Joshua came out just fine, but his mother didn't make it.

In this way, his father resented him. And he never hesitated to bring up this fact with Joshua. "I wish I could go ask Mother to make me some dinner," he would say. "But no, I can't, because you killed her!" he would taunt. Never mind that Joshua had never even had the privilege of meeting his mother. His father, Jim, was going to make Joshua pay.

It all started one morning as Joshua and a group of his friends were walking to school. They had kept up a lively conservation during the entire walk, and now the dialogue was fading. Joshua spoke up at last.

"Hey guys, what's the sour mood for? School is almost over, and then we'll be free for the summer!" At the hoots and hollers that greeted him, Joshua grinned within himself. He had always possessed the ability to lure a crowd into whatever emotion he wanted. It was a skill he thought might come in handy later. At eight years old, it seemed his shyness had finally lifted somewhat.

Jim Reynolds' plan started that very morning. In an inconceivable turn of events, Jim's friend, Tom, was a junk hauler, and someone had a bus on their property they wanted to vacate.

So, Tom grabbed his truck and went to the neighbor's house to take a look. This done, he drove the bus to his workshop, where he planned to fix it up and sell it.

Jim had other plans. "Let me borrow it," he said. "I'll leave it here the same way it is now. That is, I won't damage it in any way."

Here was where Jim's sinister plan started to unfold. Granted, it didn't appear sinister, not in the slightest. But the culmination of future events would soon change Joshua into what he was now, at fifteen, a lying, dirty, thief.

Tom let Jim borrow the bus, ("What harm could it do, anyway?") and off Jim drove in the direction of the school.

He whistled while he drove, and it wasn't long before he came upon a group of kids, which Joshua was very obviously leading. He unrolled the window and let out with a shout, "Hey kids! Need a ride?"

"Hey, that's Josh's dad!" one kid said. He turned to Joshua. "I didn't know your dad owned a bus."

Joshua gritted his teeth. "He doesn't," he muttered under his breath. But the children were already gravitating toward the bus, and Joshua had no choice but to follow.

As the last child stepped in, Jim held up his hand as Joshua climbed aboard. "No, no more room." Then, with his free hand, he pushed his son hard, into the dirt path.

Joshua was astonished as the bus drove at full-speed away. Why would his dad do such a thing to him?

He jerked himself to his feet, and started to run along the path, his backpack swaying on his shoulder. What a dirty trick, what a dirty, dirty trick...

But things didn't end there. Jim continued to pull nasty pranks on his son for his sheer enjoyment. As the years past, the pranks grew near unbearable, until Joshua could hardly stand it. Why was his father doing this to him? It wasn't fair! Jim didn't treat his eldest son, Edward, that way. Edward was Jim's pride and joy, but all Joshua was to him was a failure. A no-good, dirty, rotten failure.

So it was that Jim started having Joshua steal stuff for him. If he didn't, Jim threatened to send him away to a boy's home, and Joshua sure didn't want that. What would all his friends do without him?

The stealing began. At first it wasn't much. A candy bar, a pack of gum, and the like. But Jim's absorbency knew no bounds. Next he was asking for bigger things, like his neighbor's cat, a six-can pack of soda, and stupid stuff that Joshua could hardly bear to steal.

"I'm not a thief." he would tell himself. "I'm only doing this to save my own skin."

Which was true, in a way. But Joshua was a thief, and he would be one for the rest of his life.

Joshua spluttered from sleep, shaking at the memory. He smoothed his graying hair and looked at the clock. 3:45 in the morning. Joshua sighed, then laid back down in bed.

But he knew he wouldn't be going back to sleep. His mind would be rehashing his memories over and over until morning came.

What was the deal with all these memories crashing down upon him? Why did they control him so? He wished he had an answer.

Joshua sat up in bed and threw his legs over the side. He stood up slowly, arching his back and stretching. How old he felt. *61 isn't* that *old,* he told himself.

He walked to the bathroom and glanced at himself in the mirror. He was still trim and fit, but many years of constant stress had done a number on his emotional state.

He sighed again and walked into the kitchen. A midnight snack at 4:00 didn't sound so bad. He grabbed an apple from the fridge and took a bite. The sound was deafening. As he shuffled towards his favorite armchair, his mind went over the tasks planned for the day.

"Let's see," he said aloud. "What do I have to do today? Well, we've got Heidi's birthday, I can't forget that" he mumbled to himself. Then, with the apple hanging out of his hand, Joshua once again wrestled into a tumultuous sleep, more tired than he realized.

As Joshua walked along the streets the next morning, he wondered about what he would do when winter came. He would turn sixteen in December, and it would surely be snowing by then. He let out a sigh. When had life ever been so complicated?

When he got kicked out of his father's house, that was when. Another sigh escaped him, and he thought about what he had dreamed while lying in that crumpled heap.

He was transported back to his eighth year. When his father had started pulling nasty tricks on him. He shivered at the memory. The abuse. All the bruises.

He didn't like thinking about that time. It was too painful. So instead, he thought of the future. What he wanted to do when he was grown up.

He thought of his oratory ability. Maybe he would go into politics. Then he could become a source for good. But what about his background? With his chaotic past, he would never be elected.

Joshua trudged along the sidewalk, with no destination in mind. He would probably spend the night outdoors, in the cold. He didn't want that, but what other choice did he have? None, whatsoever. There was nothing he could do, and it made him feel weak.

Joshua spent that night under a pile of garbage to keep him warm. In a dark alley, he slept terribly until he woke up before dawn.

He felt awfully hungry and decided that his skill as a thief might actually come in handy.

He walked into a nearby general store. Lucky for him, no one seemed to be nearby. He didn't see anyone at the cash register, and as he slowly entered the store, his heart beat furiously.

When he came to the food section, he paused, and looked around once more. Seeing no one, he carefully placed a candy bar in his pocket. Looking around, he walked across the store and stole a miniature bottle of water, which he placed in his sweatshirt pocket.

Joshua nearly jumped out of his skin when he heard a loud "Hmm" behind him.

A young girl, who looked to be sixteen or seventeen, had just come out of the bathroom, arms folded across her chest, a grim expression on her face.

She held out her hand. "Okay, give it back."

Joshua didn't know what to do. He was so hungry, and he had never gotten caught before.

So he did the one thing he could think of.

He ran.

As fast as his legs could carry him, he exited the store. A race of adrenaline rushed through him. He pushed his way through the streets. He could hear the girl calling after him, "Police, stop the thief!"

Joshua dared not turn around for fear he might be slowed down.

Before he knew what was happening, he felt himself being pushed to the ground. His head hit something sharp, and he blacked out.

When Joshua woke up, he immediately recognized the police station. *Great*, he thought, *what have I gotten myself into now?*

"Good. You're awake," a voice said from behind him. He turned to see the girl who had been chasing him. Beside her was a police officer.

"Hey, boy." The officer said. "You took quite a bump on the head when I tackled you." He smiled wryly. "Sorry about that, bud."

Joshua grimaced as he rubbed his head.

The girl spoke up. "I'm Lapis." She rolled her eyes at herself. "Yes, like the metamorphic rock." She sighed.

The officer pushed some food towards Joshua. "Here, if you're desperate enough to steal, you might as well eat something."

Joshua hurriedly gobbled the burger and fries before the officer changed his mind. "What's your name, son?"

Joshua hesitated. But ended up telling the truth. "Joshua Reynolds, sir." Might as well be polite.

"Well Mr. Reynolds, this fine lady here has decided not to press charges. Now what do you think of that?"

Joshua stared wide-eyed at the girl. "Why?" he managed to say.

"Because it's just what Jesus would have done." Lapis said. "But there are a few conditions before Officer Smith here lets you go."

Ah. He knew there would be a catch. "You must come stay with me and my parents for a while, until we fatten you up and put some meat on your bones. Then, you have to promise not to steal anymore, and if you're ever hungry, you just come to us."

Joshua stood flabbergasted. "Why are you doing this?" he asked again.

"I already told you; it's what Jesus would have done. But I also feel bad for you, and I want to do something to help. So, do you agree to these conditions?"

Joshua slowly nodded his head. This had to be what he had been asking for. Had God answered his prayer?

Not that he had ever prayed to God before. He hardly knew Him. Never had formed a real relationship. Sure, God existed, but that was all.

What was this Jesus stuff about that Lapis had mentioned? Yes, Joshua was interested in that.

After a few hours, Joshua was finally released, and he walked side by side with Lapis on their way home.

"I'm just going to warn you, by family is really weird. It's just me and my mom and dad, but we have enough absurdity for eight families."

"You can't be that weird."

"Oh yeah? Well, how about this: We moved here, to Pennsylvania, from Florida, the sunshine state. Take that."

Joshua smiled ruefully. "That's not weird. A lot of families move across the country."

"That's not all. It's our name that gets me. Try to guess what our name is." Lapis grinned up at Joshua. He noticed a sparkling blue glint in her eyes.

"I'm sure I don't know. Couldn't say, that is."

"Lazuli."

"What?"

"Lazuli. That's our last name. Isn't it funny? It seems my parents had no choice but to name me Lapis because of the rock, lapis lazuli, as I mentioned earlier."

Joshua stifled a laugh. He hadn't laughed in days. "That's funny." he agreed.

"I know," Lapis intoned.

After a matter of minutes, they had arrived at the looming Lazuli household. Joshua gaped at the sheer size of the home. He had never seen a house this large before and was startled to realize he had never noticed it when walking to school or whatnot.

"Yep, this is home." said Lapis gloomily.

"Why do you say it like that?" Joshua asked, surprised at her glum manner.

"Well, when you're a part of the upper class, you tend to get liked for all the wrong reasons. Money, for one. I'm afraid I don't have any real friends because of this. Just a bunch of fakes." Lapis wrapped her arms about herself.

"Hey, I'll be your friend." Joshua could have kicked himself for what he said.

Lapis gave a dazzling smile. "I'd like that. I can tell you've had a hard upbringing, but I can also tell you're not really a bad boy. Come. I want to introduce you to my mom. My dad isn't home right now, but Mom will be happy to meet you."

"You're not really a bad boy." Those words resonated in Joshua's ears. Somehow, he believed them. Of course, he knew himself a lot better than Lapis did, but she must be right.

For all have sinned, a little voice spoke into Joshua's ear. But he ignored it and continued on his way into Lapis' grand house.

Joshua woke with a start. He looked around him, recalling the same old familiar surroundings, and gave a sigh of relief. The dreams were so *real.* Sometimes he couldn't tell the difference between fantasy and reality. He ran a hand through his quickly evaporating hair and moved to get up out of his armchair. All those memories...memories he longed to forget. He couldn't help thinking about Lapis as he went to check the time.

8:03, the clock read. "Oh, no!" Joshua thought to himself. "I'll be late for Heidi's party."

Not that he cared about the little girl. It was her mother he cared about. Rain Lyss Hawkins. Daughter of Ellyn Lyss. His sweetheart, dead approximately 24 years ago, because of his bloodthirsty cousin.

Another memory he wished he could forget.

Heidi Hawkins's party was at 9. If he could get showered and dressed in fifteen minutes, he'd have plenty of time.

After he had showered and dressed, he grabbed his car keys and headed out to his sedan.

On the way to the Hawkins', he turned on the car radio.

What he heard made him stop cold.

"Just in, looks like a bad accident. A man identified as Bob Hawkins declared dead at the hospital. Looks like a T-bone kind of affair. Poor, poor family..."

Joshua tuned out the rest. That was Heidi's dad, and Rain's husband! It couldn't be true, could it? But Bob always carried identification. "It could be another Bob Hawkins." Joshua reasoned out loud. But something in his gut told him he was wrong.

Bob was dead.

On the way to his daughter's birthday party.

Joshua cringed. He only hoped he wouldn't be the one to break the news.

There was good news and bad news. The good news was Joshua didn't have to tell the Hawkins family about the accident.

The bad news was they already knew.

Heidi was clinging desperately to her mother, Rain, who was sobbing uncontrollably. She held baby Isabelle in her lap and was rocking back and forth.

Long time friends Teresa Morgan and Angelina Carmen stood nearby, clutching each other in their arms. They were thinking about their families, and what they would do if one of their husbands was killed.

"First my grandmother, and now this," Rain was saying when Joshua walked in. "And on poor Heidi's birthday, too."

Angelina was speaking in low tones to Teresa. "You know I'm a detective, and I'm telling you, something's not right here."

"Of course it isn't right!" Rain sobbed. "My husband is dead, and it's all God's fault!"

Joshua heard Heidi speak up for the first time. "Of course it isn't God's fault, Mom. God has a purpose for everything He does." Baby Isabelle began to wail, and Rain held her small daughter tighter.

"Of course this is His fault. You think I wanted this? I've done nothing but serve God for the past two years, and this is how He repays me? No, this is it. I'm done. Done with You, God, and done with life."

She wretched baby Isabelle out of her arms and raced to the kitchen. Angelina quickly took action as she heard the kitchen knife drawer, punctuated by a little squeak, open and slam close. She raced into the kitchen to discover she was too late. Rain's very lifeblood was bleeding out onto the linoleum floor.

LAPIS TUGGED AT JOSHUA'S arm, smiling gaily. He walked beside her, hand in pocket, and grinned self-consciously to himself.

It had been four years since they had met, and much had happened in those four years.

Joshua had a chance to meet Lapis' parents, and he spent three months in rehabilitation there. He had never eaten so well and felt so good.

Joshua returned to school and finished his senior year with honors. After that, he decided to become an architect. Lapis also finished and chose to become an aquatic reynologist.

Now, here they were, both in college, and living the dream of their lives, with God by their side.

Lapis continued to tug Joshua's arm. She giggled flirtatiously and they continued to climb the steep hill with dexterity.

When they finally reached the top, Lapis fell into Joshua's arms. Together, they held each other as they took in the gorgeous panoramic view.

Figuring this was as good a time as any, Joshua stooped to one knee and asked her to marry him.

"Yes!!!" Lapis exclaimed, and she leapt into his arms. Teasingly, she said, "Now I won't be Lapis Lazuli anymore!"

So it was, that, in the following months, they were married. It was a joyous occasion for all involved, and Joshua had never felt happier.

That was before the accident, occurring just a few months after the Reynolds' honeymoon.

It was a normal day. Both Joshua and Lapis were working on their homework outside.

The images came in mini collages. The smell of smoke. The sight of their beautiful house, funded by Lapis' parents, burning. Lapis rushing inside to grab her most important thing, namely her Bible.

And never coming back out.

It was later confirmed that the cause of the fire was a small case of matches and a good deal of gasoline.

Joshua had his suspicions, but it wasn't until he walked up to his father's house that he knew.

His father was gone. The pick-up truck was revving out of the driveway by the time Joshua arrived, and he didn't have the energy to trail his father.

His father had done this. Killed his beloved Lapis, the only beautiful gem of his short life.

He considered ending himself but decided against it. There was too much to live for in this world. God, for one. He couldn't give up on God.

So, suicide was out of the question. But what should he do? What should he do....?

Joshua tugged himself back into the present. Blood, so much of it, was draining away from Rain and onto the floor.

Teresa, in command, shouted, "Someone call 911! And hurry!" Angelina immediately removed her phone from her pocket and set to work.

Meanwhile, Teresa had grabbed a towel off the kitchen sink and was applying constant pressure to the knife wound.

Heidi, pale as a ghost, took in the whole affair with Isabelle in her arms. Joshua walked over to her, placing a comforting hand upon her shoulder.

She looked up with frightened eyes, then relaxed when she saw it was Joshua standing there.

"Mr. Joshua," she said placidly, "what's going on? I don't understand."

She's in shock, Joshua realized. He did his best to comfort the girl. "Your mother's in a bit of trouble." he started. Well, he wasn't one to sugarcoat things. "She's had a terrible shock, and she just couldn't take it."

"But Mom is the strongest person I know. Besides Daddy, that is. Where is Daddy? It's my eighth birthday. I'm turning eight..." she trailed off, a look of confusion on her face.

Joshua grappled with fear at telling the truth to this child. "Your father, he, that is to say, he's, not coming back."

"What do you mean? Of course he is."

"No, I'm afraid not."

"Is this what Mommy was so upset about? That made her want to hurt herself? That's always made her want to hurt herself?"

Joshua winced. Maybe Rain was more traumatized by it all more than he had realized.

Suddenly Heidi let out a piercing shriek. "My daddy's dead! He's dead!" She continued to intone the words over and over, until a dull throb took over body, and she began to shake.

Joshua wrapped his arms around the little girl.

By this time, emergency personnel had arrived, and they were escorting Rain's lifeless body into the back of the ambulance.

Joshua allowed short sobs to overtake him. A distinct memory washed over him. How nearly twenty-eight years ago, he made a promise. A solemn promise to Ellyn Lyss that he would watch over Rain the best he could, if anything should ever happen to Ellyn, so she could no longer take care of her daughter.

So far he had fulfilled that obligation, but now, now all was lost.

He was a devastated man who couldn't keep his promises.

A failure. Just like his father said.

The emotion was gripping. He felt he needed to be there for the family, but suddenly he felt dragged back into the past.

At the extreme loss at losing Lapis. Joshua was thrown back into the throes of life. He quit college, started drinking, and never went to church.

His life was in shambles, to put it simply. He had never made anything of his life, and he never would. He was a failure at everything he did. Life didn't matter anymore.

It only grew worse when he had to face his father before a court.

As Jim Reynolds was sentenced, Joshua couldn't get a hold on himself. So finally, he had to leave.

As he was walking out, his father and he caught each other's gaze. There was a measure of hate in the eyes of the father, but there was also something else. Satisfaction, maybe. At seeing everything his son loved die.

Joshua fought back tears as he passed through the corridors, rubbing his hands against his eyes. This was all a dream, and he would wake up.

But this wasn't a dream. It was a nightmare. And it would never end. Ever.

Joshua shook his head to regain his bearings. The little girl was still there, sobbing softly, and Joshua thought about how utterly alone she was. It depressed him, really, to see how alone she really was.

It created a parallel between the two of them. The loneliness Joshua felt after losing Lapis, the pain and anger and regret Heidi was sure to feel at the loss of both her parents on the same day.

The one, a terrible accident that could probably have been avoided. Though, knowing Angelina, who thought nothing was an accident, would probably try to investigate Bob Hawkins' death and deduce foul play.

But the other, a suicide by a Christian woman who seemed to have faith in God, but apparently didn't seem to have enough.

It *was* depressing, all of it. His emotion came in waves of heaving sobs, to barely masked grunts of attempts to hold the sentiment at bay.

He looked back at Heidi. She was grasping Isabelle tightly in her arms, and the baby had calmed down somewhat.

Joshua laid a hand across her face, surprised at her cold temperature. He could feel perspiration pouring down his own back, but the only sweat on her little face was that of the tears draining from her eyes.

That night, Joshua ran over the rest of the afternoon in his head. He couldn't stop thinking about Rain, and how tragically her life had ended. If only he could go back and fix all of it, then everything would be different.

A knock on the door startled him out of his reverie. "Open up, Reynolds!" someone shouted.

Joshua ran to the door, fumbled with the lock, and finally had the door open. It was his landlord.

With an eviction notice.

"Get out of here in a week, Reynolds." he snarled. "And it'll be too soon," he muttered more to himself than anyone else.

Joshua took the sheet of paper that was ending his life as he knew it.

And crumpled into a heap and cried.

Why had God thrown him another curveball of life? What did he do to deserve this?

He could imagine Lapis speaking, in soothing tones, *"He's testing you, Joshua. He'll never give you more than you can bear."*

Gritting his teeth, Joshua ripped the eviction notice into tiny pieces.

None of this would have happened if he hadn't been born. Maybe he should end it all, just as Rain had done.

But no, he couldn't do that. He needed to help Heidi now. And get to the bottom of whatever Angelina was saying about foul play.

As he watched the world around him collapse on itself, he made a solemn vow.

Where he had failed Rain, he would not fail Heidi.

He would be her silent guardian, watching over her from afar. He would have to do it without arousing suspicion, but he felt it was something he needed to do to gain closure on all of this.

Because doubtless the blood splattered on the linoleum floor would be in his nightmares tonight.

The nightmares came in full force that night. Never had he wanted to drink so badly. But he stopped himself. He wouldn't go down that road again. No, not for anything.

So he spent that night, willing himself to fall asleep, but to no avail.

In the morning, he drove directly to the Morgan home, where Heidi and Isabelle had been staying the night.

He knocked on the door cautiously. He could see the outline of Heidi as she rose to answer the door. Teresa trailed after her, carrying baby Isabelle in her arms.

Heidi reached the door first, opening it. When she saw Joshua standing there, she immediately grasped him in a fierce hug.

He didn't know what to say, and he looked to Teresa for help. She shook her head. *Let her,* she mouthed.

So, Joshua did. He returned to her embrace, gradually lowering himself to her level.

"My parents are dead," she pronounced clearly. "But God is going to take care of me." She looked up at the ceiling. "Aren't You, God?" She nodded her approval.

Joshua was amazed at her faith. And grimaced when he thought of where his faith had been when he lost Lapis.

Maybe they weren't so alike after all.

"Let Mr. Joshua come in," Teresa said, and Heidi emerged from the hug. She took Joshua by the hand and led him into the living room.

"No, that's alright." Joshua shuffled his feet. "I just wanted to make sure Heidi was okay." He looked at Teresa. "I got evicted from my apartment today, so it looks like I'm back on the streets."

He didn't know why he was telling her all this. It benefited him nothing.

"I'll pray for you." Teresa smiled at him sweetly, and he saw something of Lapis in that smile. He choked on his next words.

"Thanks. I've got to go."

He rushed out the door, away from memories that threatened to constrict his very being.

Chapter 2

Joshua climbed into his sedan and began the trek back home. He wasn't looking forward to it, that was for sure.

It was a good twenty minutes from his apartment, and Joshua relished the time he had alone in his car. As he pulled up to a stop sign, he noticed a homeless man on the side of the street, with his thumb out, asking for a ride.

Will that be me in a couple of weeks? Joshua questioned himself. He hoped not.

But it made Joshua think. And have compassion. He slowly drove into a nearby parking lot and motioned for the man to join him in the car.

"God bless you, sir!" The man exclaimed, as he fastened his seat belt.

"No problem," Joshua mumbled. "Where do you want to go?" he asked nonchalantly.

"Oh, wherever you were going before you picked me up would be fine." The man said eloquently. "I just needed a ride to give you this." He held out a battered and worn old watch.

Joshua smiled to himself. So, this was a nut. In his car. Great.

"Oh no, that's all right." Joshua said demurely. "Say, what's your name anyway?" he asked.

"The name's Peter, and this watch is for you." Peter lowered his voice to a whisper. "You see, this isn't any ordinary watch. This, my good friend, is a time machine."

The air left Joshua's lungs. Wow, this guy *was* crazy.

The two talked on, and Joshua was surprised to see himself pulling into his apartment building complex.

As the two got out, Peter handed Joshua the watch. "I know you think I'm crazy, I can see it in your eyes," he added. "But trust me, this powerful device isn't magic. It's *real*.

And it could solve all your problems."

"Then why are you giving it to me?" Joshua blurted.

"Because you showed kindness to an old man like me. I'm simply repaying you for your goodwill."

"Thanks?" Joshua glanced down at the watch. He looked up to see the man already gone, heading back into the direction where they had just come. "Silly old man," Joshua mumbled to himself.

He got out of the sedan and walked up to his apartment. Once there, he debated what he should do with the watch. If he cleaned it up real nicely, he could probably pawn it off somewhere.

But maybe what the man said was partly true. Of course, not the time travel part; that was nonsense. But maybe he was still capable of demonstrating kindness to others. He wasn't old enough to be a grouch yet. That was progress in the right direction.

When Joshua arrived at his apartment, he immediately set his things down, and went to badger his boss for empty boxes he always had laying around.

That done, he began packing up his stuff.

Joshua was a strict minimalist, and in a matter of hours, his most valuable possessions had been packed up and placed in a corner of the room.

Resting in his favorite armchair, Joshua removed the watch from his pocket. His thoughts wandered to the first present Lapis had ever given him: a watch most similar to this one.

He caressed the watch soothingly, wondering where Lapis' watch was. He hadn't seen it while packing today, but most assuredly it was here somewhere.

Thinking about Lapis always made his heart hurt, and he longed to forget. But he couldn't.

He rubbed the watch more ferociously, as a calming effect. However, the exact opposite was true, and everything began to spin...

Joshua couldn't believe his eyes. This had to be a dream.

He found himself in a briar bush, watching a scene only too familiar unfold.

He heard Lapis giggling as she handed him, a younger, more youthful Joshua, a brilliantly shining watch.

Joshua was flabbergasted, to say the least. He dared not make himself known and stared down at the old watch in his hands.

How was he here? Was time travel possible? How could this be happening? He wracked his brain in an attempt to figure out just how he got here.

He watched younger Joshua and Lapis grasp each other's hands as they walked away and felt a sinking feeling within himself.

In a dream, he could just will himself awake, and he would return to reality. But pinch himself as he might, no cloudy image blurred, and he was still here.

The most important question on his mind: How had he got here? And how could he leave? And, more importantly, was Peter, the old homeless man, right?

Was time travel real?

What had he been doing before he was transported here? He forced himself to think. He had been reminiscing, that was it, thinking about the past. And he had been...rubbing the watch! Was that how he got here?

Earnestly, desperately, he caressed the watch, wishing with all his might he could go home. He pictured it in his mind, the sight of his beloved apartment, which he was sure to lose in a matter of days.

A spinning sensation ensued, and suddenly he found himself in his armchair, just like where he had been before.

He slowed his dizzying heart rate, and his breath came in short gasps.

What just happened? he asked himself. What in the world was going on?

As he slowed his breathing, he thought of the power he now held within his grasp. At first, he wanted to get rid of the thing. He probably had the power to change the course of history, just as Peter had been telling him. Or rather, *warning* him.

Joshua groaned within himself. What was he going to do?

He was startled when an idea came to him.

He could keep everyone he loved and cared about from dying. Lapis, Rain, Bob.

He nearly choked on the name. Ellyn. He could save Ellyn from his cousin. He could even save his cousin from killing herself!

Joshua was astounded by how many people in his life had passed away. But he could change all that. He knew he could.

He thought about what was going to happen when he changed the lives of so many people. And whoever he cared about would be saved first. The choices were easy.

It had to be Lapis or Ellyn. The two women he cared most about.

He sighed within himself. Maybe the choices weren't so easy.

No. It would have to be Lapis. Lapis was his first love, though not his last. He remembered how his dear Lapis had died. She had run into the burning house to rescue her Bible. Well, he would just have to convince her it wasn't worth it.

But how? Lapis loved her Bible more than anything. Sometimes, he thought, even more than she loved him.

But, back then, he had loved his Bible too. He just wasn't willing to risk his life over some dusty old book. No, he had never had the faith Lapis did. He cringed at the thought.

Another thing he had to consider was the fact that he couldn't actually speak to Lapis. He would have to speak to the younger version of himself.

He should probably arrive a few hours early, just to ensure that everything went off smoothly and without a hitch.

Maybe, instead of having his past self persuade Lapis into not going back inside, he could confront his father before the fire ever started.

Yes, that was a better plan.

With all his might, he rubbed the watch, imagining just where he wanted to be. Just what he wanted to do. He felt a familiar spin...

...Then he was in the grocery store, where he had been shopping a few hours before the fire.

He immediately noticed himself looking over the canned food. "Joshua," he whispered, attempting to disguise his voice. Why, he didn't know. Young Joshua was sure to recognize him anyway.

Young Joshua looked up from his shopping, and Joshua whispered, "Over here, on the aisle across from you."

Young Joshua immediately made his way over to where Joshua lay in wait. "Did someone call my name?" he asked aloud. Before he saw Joshua kneeling there.

"What in the world?" Young Joshua muttered to himself. Before catching a glimpse of Joshua's face.

He appeared about to shout, but Joshua stopped him, grasping his wrists and putting his hand across his mouth.

"Don't say a word," Joshua warned. "I know you're confused, but just listen, okay?" He released young Joshua's mouth.

Young Joshua crossed his arms over his chest, a look of shock mixed with stubbornness etched across his face. "You're just a creepy old man, right?" he asked. "Who also happens to look a lot like me."

"No," Joshua said. "I *am* you. I know this is really cheesy, but I've come from the future, to warn you, about something."

"What in the world?" Young Joshua looked like he was about to faint. "I must be losing my mind." He half-giggled. "That's it, I'm going crazy."

He looked back at Joshua. "What do you need to tell me, future self?"

Joshua slapped his young counterpart's wrist. "This isn't a game, Josh." He spoke. "I've come from the future because Lapis is going to die today, and you have to stop it."

"What?!" Young Joshua said.

"It's true. Your dad-our dad-is going to start a fire at your house. Lapis is going to go back in for her Bible, but you can't let her. She never comes back out."

"Why should I believe you?"

"Because I want a future with Lapis, and I'm leaving it up to you to save her. Please, bear with me."

Young Joshua still didn't know what to say. "Okay." He swallowed. "I'll do what you say, but how?"

Joshua had been thinking about this, and he said, "Just do whatever you have to. Grab her and don't let go if you must. Whatever it takes. Just don't let Lapis go back in there. If she does, she will die."

"So, what are you going to do? Just go back to your little fairyland and wait for Lapis to appear before you?"

"No, I'll stick it out here, and make sure nothing goes wrong. Meanwhile, I'll be trying to keep Dad from starting the fire in the first place."

"Wait, why would Dad want to start a fire on our house?"

"Because" Joshua said grimly, "Dad always wanted what we had. A loving wife. A beautiful home. If he could take those things away, then he thought he would feel better."

"How are you going to stop him?" Young Joshua asked.

Joshua shook his head. "Not sure yet. I'll find a way."

"You better. I don't think I can restrain Lapis for long. You know how she is."

"Yeah." Joshua made his way toward the exit of the grocery store.

"I'll see you in a few hours, then?" Young Joshua called.

"You bet." Joshua vociferated over his shoulder.

Try as he might, Joshua couldn't find Jim Reynolds, his dad, anywhere. He had limited transportation, and walking for long stretches at a time wasn't fun for a sixty-one-year-old.

Finally, Joshua resigned himself to wait at the house until his father arrived. He remembered from past police reports that the fire had started from the back, and he resigned himself to wait back there for his father to arrive.

It seemed like hours, but in reality, it was only an hour or so before Jim Reynolds arrived, toting a box of matches and a can of gasoline.

Joshua waited for his father to notice him. When he did, he gave a shocked cry of surprise.

"Why, I didn't know anyone was back here." He stammered. "I was just, ah, going to, ah."

"Burn the house down?" Joshua questioned with a grimace.

"Of, of course not," Jim spluttered. "This is private property, you know. I'm telling you to get off."

"Oh really?" Joshua rolled his eyes. "And, uh, what are you planning to do with that gasoline and those matches, huh? Why don't you give them here." Joshua lunged for the matches, but missed.

However, it gave Jim a good chance to investigate his son's face. After regaining a passive expression after his formidable shock, he gave a hard grin.

"So, either I'm dreaming or you're my son from the future, is that right? Coming to take down your old man?"

Joshua was astonished at his father's synopsis. He didn't let it show. "That's right, Jim," he said, using his father's first name, for no other reason but that he could.

"Then's lets fight." Jim said, unscrewing the gas cap from the can of gasoline. "It's not like you can stop me. The past can't be changed, you know."

They circled each other, and Jim began slowly dousing the house with gas.

"I wouldn't do that if I were you," Joshua growled.

"Too late," Jim said, and he struck a match.

Joshua pushed Jim to the ground before he could throw the match at the house. "Oh no you don't," he muttered through gritted teeth.

The two wrestled on the ground for several moments, with Joshua obviously proving the victor.

But he must have let his guard down, for Jim managed to strike another match. He threw it at the house, which immediately burst into flames.

"No!!!" Joshua shouted, and he rammed himself into his father. "You're ruining everything!" he screamed.

He shoved Jim to the ground and raced to the front of the house.

"Joshua!" He hollered as loud as he could. "Don't let Lapis into the house! The fire's started; I'm going to try to put it out."

Young Joshua immediately grabbed Lapis and held her tightly. "Let go!" He could hear Lapis screaming. "I need to get something important."

"Don't let her go!" Joshua yelled.

"I won't!" Young Joshua yelled back.

Joshua raced to the back of the house, where his father had disappeared. Grabbing a bucket from nearby, he raced down to the creek that ran the length of the house.

He already knew it was a lost cause.

The house was burning, and the firemen would never be able to arrive fast enough.

He let the bucket drop from his hands, before bowing to his knees.

"Thank you, God, for saving Lapis for me," he prayed. As he stood to his feet, he heard yelling.

"Lapis, no! You can't go in there!"

Joshua gasped, as he headed back around to the front of the house. By now, the flames were so hot it was a wonder how Lapis ever managed to get inside.

But she was in the house before Joshua ever made it to the front. As the house burned, Joshua turned with hatred on his younger self.

"How could you?" He yelled. "I told you to keep her secure! Now she's lost to me forever." He shoved young Joshua to the ground, before falling to the ground himself and weeping over all that he had lost. For a second time.

"Look man, I'm sorry." Young Joshua was crying as well. "I tried not to let her go, but she escaped somehow."

"Don't make excuses," Joshua sighed. It was all over now. He hadn't been able to save Lapis. Again. He was a failure.

Slowly he took the watch out of his pocket. He caressed it softly, imagining himself in his armchair back home, and without a backward glance, vanished from young Joshua's sight, leaving him to mourn alone, the sound of sirens echoing in the distance.

Joshua was back in his armchair, sobbing loudly, weeping as he reexperienced the treacherous memories of poor Lapis' body going up into flames.

He heard a knocking on the door and managed to whisk most of the tears away from his face as he got up from his armchair.

"Coming," he called, his voice muffled by the sound of sobs. As he opened his door, he saw his landlord. He wore a rare compassionate face and he spoke gently.

"Another PTSD episode, huh?" he asked benignly.

At Joshua's nod, he approached the topic of business. "All right, because I feel sorry for you, and what happened to your," he paused, with an ahem, "friend, I see fit to give you an extra week." He shuffled, placing his hand in his pockets, then wiping them against his shirt. He wasn't used to positive confrontation with one of his tenants.

"So, there's that," he said, and walked off. "Call me if you need any more boxes."

It took Joshua a second to realize who his landlord was talking about when he said "friend." Then he realized that he obviously meant Rain. Her death had been all over the news. Maybe he could save her. But somehow, he doubted it. If Rain didn't kill herself then, she would kill herself later. No, the solution was to save Bob, so Rain wouldn't feel the need to take her own life.

In order to find information about Bob, there was only one person Joshua knew to go to.

Angelina.

Angelina Carmen was a detective who had even interrogated him, once. She knew her stuff, and her comments at Heidi's birthday party seemed proof of that. Her suspicions of foul play made everything change.

Joshua needed to figure out where Bob was, and why, and he needed to find some way to keep this whole fiasco from taking place.

He needed to know the exact details of everything that had happened that day. Why someone might have wanted Bob dead, and how Bob's death had occurred.

Sure, the news reporter on the radio said it was a T-bone incident, but were people on the radio really that reliable? Joshua thought not.

However, he knew he could get all these answers from Angelina, and he intended to do just that.

Nothing would get in the way of his saving Bob. And then, most importantly, he could save his sweetheart, Ellyn Lyss.

Chapter 3

Angelina was a wealth of information. In the small town of Huntsville, Pennsylvania, she knew a little bit of everything about everyone.

Joshua wasn't surprised she was interested in the Hawkins' case. Being a long-time family friend in some strange way, (Joshua wasn't exactly sure of the story) gave Angelina a keen interest in the Hawkins family.

There had been stories about how Angelina had become so personally involved in the Hawkins' business. It all started with Ellyn Lyss, of course.

Joshua paused in his reverie and sighed. Oh, how he missed his Ellyn.

Ellyn Lyss had been walking in the rain one day, Joshua didn't know why, perhaps a sudden storm had arisen.

In fact, that seemed to be the case, for, as the story went, rain was coming down in torrents. In the vast downpour, Ellyn crossed the road, only to be hit by a car.

Joshua surprised himself at how much he knew. He went on in his head.

It seems Angelina called the ambulance that would later save Ellyn's life. And the life of the baby inside her, Rain.

After Ellyn recovered, the two became fast friends.

Or that was how the story went.

Either way, it didn't really matter. The point was, Joshua could trust Angelina.

So, back at her office, Angelina was producing a spat of evidence that gave reason to the fact that Bob's death hadn't been accidental.

It was murder.

Angelina had led her investigation well. She had concluded a most alluring hypothesis, and she shared it with Joshua now.

"From the summary I gave earlier," she started, "We can all surmise that Bob may have been in quite a lot of debt."

"May have been?" Joshua grimaced. "From what you showed me, there's no question about it."

"That may be true." Angelina shoved her hair out of her face. "So, my hypothesis goes like this. Bob's in a lot of debt. So much debt that this banker dude doesn't think it will ever get paid back.

"So, he concocts a plan that would give him the money from the life insurance policy on Bob. He'd threaten Rain, and get it that way. Thing is, Rain knew nothing about the debt."

"That throws a monkey wrench into things, doesn't it?" Joshua said.

Angelina nodded. "That it does. So, we have evidence of a carjacking. We just have to lay it on this Mr. Fritz, the name of the banker."

"Isn't this all supposed to be confidential?"

"Well, it's supposed to be, and I really shouldn't be sharing with you everything that I just have. Especially if I've got it all wrong. So, let's just keep this to ourselves, all right?"

Joshua agreed. Now he had some questions.

"Any idea what the car looked like?"

"Oh sure, I've got it right here." She looked at him sternly. "Promise you won't tell anyone? I'm only telling you because you're such a close friend to the Hawkins family. Aren't you supposed to be Heidi's legal guardian now?"

That was new, but back to the point. "The car?" he prodded Angelina softly.

"Sure, sure. It's a Honda civic, a vermilion color." She gave him the license plate number.

"You know the exact time of the carjacking? And how it went down?"

Angelina gave him an odd look. "Curious one, aren't you? Well, I can tell you that as well. Around 8:00 in the morning, maybe 8:30 at the latest. A bomb was planted underneath the car's axle. Then, a hitman came in and finished the job, just in case the bomb didn't go off, or was found before and disengaged."

"The hitman t-boned the car?"

"Looks like it."

"So, pay off the hitman, and disentangle the bomb. Okay, I can do that."

Angelina looked at him curiously. "What are you talking about? There's nothing you can do."

Joshua smiled. A real, honest to goodness smile. "I have my ways." He briefly debated within himself whether he should go through with this or not.

Finally decided that this was the best way, he produced the watch from his pants pocket.

Angelina gave him the *are you crazy* look. "You can't change the past, Josh."

Joshua smiled again. "Or can I?" he said. "You know how to dismantle a bomb?"

"Well sure, but..." she trailed off, looking at him quizzically. "What are you up to, anyway?"

"Stand up." Joshua ordered. She did so, as did he. "Take my hand." He spoke his words carefully.

"What's going on, what are you doing?"

But Joshua didn't answer. He was already rubbing the watch furtively, thinking in his mind just where he wanted to be. Then the room began to spin.

When he opened his eyes, he found himself at Bob's workplace, a lumberyard not fifteen minutes away from the Hawkins home.

Joshua could see Angelina visibly shaking. "What in the world?" she said breathlessly. "How are we here? What...?" her words trailed off, and she looked to Joshua for guidance.

"We're in the past. A couple hours before Heidi's party. He looked at the watch. "Approximately 5:30." He spoke.

Angelina made a tug at her hair. "But how?" she asked,

still unbelieving.

"Truly simple, really. I have only to rub this watch and imagine where I want to be, and boom, I'm there."

"I can't believe this isn't a dream."

"Well, I can. And we have a lot of work to do, so let's

get to it."

"Work? What work?" Angelina asked cautiously.

"You said you knew how to disengage a bomb, right? So, let's go." Joshua made his way over to the parking lot, and spotted Bob's car. When they arrived, Angelina immediately set to work.

"How'd you know what tools I needed?" she asked.

"Simple. Asked my landlord. He's done a little bit of everything."

"So, what are you going to do?"

"Track down that hitman. Pay him off if necessary."

"Where are you going to get the money? Didn't you just lose your apartment?" Angelina muttered the last words at a low whisper, but Joshua still heard it.

"Got some money saved up," he offered as an appropriate response.

"So how are you going to get wherever you need to go?" Angelina posed a plausible question.

Joshua hadn't thought of that. "I'll find a ride somewhere."

He was off, running as fast as his sixty-one-year-old body could carry him. He held his finger out, as he ran, hoping for a ride. He needed to get to the bank, a few miles from here.

Hopefully he could find the banker, Mr. Fritz, and give him the payments Bob so desperately owed. He had no idea how much Bob owed, but maybe a small percentage of that could be glazed over. At least for a little while.

As it turned out, Joshua jogged the whole way. He felt confident in his plan. Angelina was detaching the bomb, which she had immediately found underneath the car.

If he could get Mr. Fritz to agree with his foolhardy plan, he wouldn't need to track down the hitman.

Like that was possible anyway.

As Joshua rushed into the lobby of the bank, he was met with some strange covert glances. Normally this would have bothered him, but today he didn't care.

As luck would have it, there was no one waiting in line and Joshua was up.

"How can I help you?" The young woman with the name tag of Amber said.

"I'd like to speak to a Mr. Fritz, if I may." Joshua still found himself huffing and puffing for breath.

"Of course. He's in a meeting right now, but he doesn't have any appointments lined up after that. Would you like to come back, or wait here, or—"

"Look lady, this is kind of an emergency. Like, life and death. Would you kindly get him for me?" Joshua pressed his palms against the cold marble of Amber's desk.

She gave him a worried expression. "Of course, if it's a real emergency..." She trailed off.

Amber stood up. I'll be with you in just a moment. Please wait in the lobby."

She walked away, and Joshua took a seat on a plush couch in the center of the room.

But he couldn't stay down. Soon he was pacing back and forth, waiting for Amber to return.

Soon, she did. With two security guards. Amber cast Joshua a sympathetic smile. "I'm sorry, sir. But I couldn't let you disturb Mr. Fritz and his important meeting. These two guards are going to have to escort you out. I'm sorry."

Joshua pushed back against the officers restraining. "No, you don't understand. This really is an emergency."

Somehow, he managed to push past them and dove for the meeting room. Just as his hand reached the knob, he felt his body go limp and a needle-sharp pain echoed through his veins. "Now, wait a minute," he said, before slumping to the ground.

Joshua woke up to the sound of a radio playing.

"Just in, looks like a bad accident. A man identified as Bob Hawkins..." Joshua tuned out the rest. So. He had failed. Just like he had failed Lapis. For the second time.

Joshua took in his surroundings. A hospital, by the looks of it.

A psychiatric hospital, Joshua realized. *They think I'm crazy, and now Bob's dead.*

He needed to get out of here. And fast. But he couldn't leave Angelina here alone. She might meet her past self and who knew what the two of them might get into.

He was strapped down. That was the bad news. The good news was, the watch was in plain sight, and within his reach. So, how could he get out of this mess?

Well, first he needed to contact Angelina. He pressed the little button sitting on the side of the bed.

A woman showed up almost immediately. "Hello, you're awake!" she said, too cheerfully. "I'm Emmy, and I'll be taking care of you today. Now, you called? What do you need?"

"I need to call someone." Joshua mumbled. "Can I borrow the phone?"

"Sure." She reached over him and grabbed the phone from the bedside table. "Who do you need to call? Family?"

"No. A friend." Joshua said. "Someone who'll get me out of here." He mumbled to himself.

Emmy didn't appear to notice. "You don't mind if I listen in, do you?"

"Sure. Do whatever you want." Good thing he made himself memorize all his friends' phone numbers.

Angelina picked up on the first ring. "Joshua, is that you? I removed the bomb and I've been waiting at the bank for ages. What happened? Where are you?"

"Long story." Joshua said. "I'm at Huntsville Psychiatric Hospital."

"Where Ellyn worked?" A pause. Then an apology. "Sorry, I didn't mean to bring that up."

"It's fine." Joshua grimaced; impatience written on his face. "Look, can you get me out of here, please?" he whispered.

"Sure, sure." Angelina huffed. He could hear her scrambling up from her seat and leaving the bank.

"I heard the radio in here." She said in a quiet voice. "Sounds like Bob didn't make it, huh?"

"No." The simple monosyllable took all of Joshua's energy to drag out.

"All right. I'll be there in a few."

In truth, it was a little less than an hour until Angelina arrived. Obviously, she hadn't been able to find a ride.

She sauntered in slowly, as if she had nowhere else to be. Emmy was in a corner, watching furtively.

"How'd you manage to get yourself locked up in this place, huh, old boy?" Angelina asked in her usual carefree way.

Joshua could see her make a quick sweep of the room, her eyes instantly landing on the watch.

She grasped it in her hand, slowly started rubbing it, and grasped Joshua's clothes. Joshua noticed for the first time he was wearing hospital scrubs.

Joshua grasped Angelina's arm, and the two looked at Emmy respectively. "Bye," they said in unison and suddenly they were gone.

Emmy sat in her chair, dumbfounded. Then she immediately called the other nurses for help.

Joshua and Angelina were immediately transported back to her office.

Angelina sat in her chair.

"Well, that mission was a failure," she said despondently.

Failure. A word that seemed to punctuate Joshua's life at every turn. He sighed audibly.

"So, do we go back and try again?" Angelina asked innocently.

Joshua shook her head. "No, no, we can't do that. We need to move on to the next thing."

"Which is what?" Angelina asked.

Joshua then proceeded to tell Angelina about his encounter with his dual self, the outcome that followed, and the loss of Lapis for the second time.

After Joshua finished his commentary, Angelina spoke up. "So...if you've failed twice already, what's to say the past can't be manipulated? What if God's destined everything to happen in His own way, and us trifling with it makes Him angry?"

"God never wanted sin to enter into the world." He continued. "So now we need to keep Rain from killing herself."

The full gravity of their now newly possessed power overwhelmed Angelina for a second. "But what if that doesn't work? What if Rain still kills herself despite our efforts?"

"We have to try," Joshua amended.

Angelina exhaled. "So, how are we going to pull this off? And, unless I'm mistaken, how are we going to convince our doubles to stay away?"

Joshua rubbed his chin. "I'm not quite sure. I was hoping you would have some ideas."

Angelina smiled grimly. "Oh, I have a few, but none that you're going to like." She started to whisper in his ear.

"Why, that's crazy!" Joshua exclaimed.

Angelina nodded. "I know, but it's the only thing I can come up with."

Joshua sighed. "All right, let me think it over. I'll get back to you in the morning." He scratched the hair on his head.

Angelina gave him a confused look. "Shouldn't we do this now? I mean, I don't really know how time travel works, but something tells me we shouldn't wait."

"Why? Because Rain's funeral will take place in a few days? No, we'll get her back before that, and that funeral will never happen."

"How can you be so sure? We've failed once already."

"Trust me, we're not going to fail this time."

That evening, after pulling a microwave dinner out of the freezer and eating it, Joshua sat staring at the watch. How could time travel be possible, anyway?

Maybe this was all a dream. But somehow Joshua knew it wasn't. Everything was far too real.

Putting the watch down, Joshua allowed himself to think about Lapis. The sweet, beautiful woman he had lost all those years ago.

He remembered when they first met, him being so hungry that he was required to steal.

And then she had invited him to her house. As a type of rehabilitation process.

Man, did he miss her.

Then he thought about Bob. Poor guy. Joshua hadn't been able to save him either. He pounded his fist into the armrest of his chair.

He recalled how many times he had heard his father call him a failure, and now he knew for sure it was true.

But he wouldn't fail Rain. He couldn't fail Ellyn, either. He needed to save them both.

But first things first. He needed to get a good night's sleep tonight so he would be prepared tomorrow morning.

He and Angelina had a job to do, and Joshua had no intent to fail.

Joshua barely slept that night. He had too many thoughts running through his head. Angelina's plan was crazy, but Joshua had no better idea. He recounted her whispered words in his mind.

"The only thing I can think of," she had said. "We kidnap our doubles and take their place."

"Why can't we just talk to them reasonably?" Joshua had asked.

Angelina rolled her eyes. "You really think I would listen to my look-alike? I don't think so."

"How would we do it? How would we keep them from escaping?"

"Easy, tie them up and put them in the back of your car."

"Why my car?"

"Because it's bigger, that's why." Angelina gave an impatient shrug of her shoulders. "Look, if you have a better idea, please let me know."

"I'll sleep on it." Joshua had said. So far, he hadn't been able to come up with a better plan. Other than the fact he'd rather talk to his double than kidnap and tie him up on the spot.

Maybe he would be more reasonable than Angelina's double.

When Joshua walked into Angelina's office that morning, watch in his coat pocket, she was already standing and ready to go.

"You think of any better ideas?" she asked immediately.

"Only that I think we should try to talk to them first."

"Fine. Suits me." Angelina said carelessly. "So, are we going to do this, or what?"

Joshua pulled out the watch. Together, they grasped each other's hands, and Joshua imagined just where he wanted to be. The room began to spin, and instantly they found themselves outside Joshua's apartment.

"Why'd you bring us here?" Angelina demanded. "What time is it?"

Joshua checked the watch. "8:30, or somewhere around there. I'm about to leave for Heidi's party."

"So, your plan is to convince your past self not to go to the party, and let you go in your place?" She made a confused expression. "Wow, that didn't make any sense."

"Well, at least you get the gist of it." Joshua said.

"So, what am I supposed to do while you're in there?"

"Wait, I guess. I'd really rather you weren't part of this at all." Joshua looked into Angelina's eyes. "It's important that we do this right. And I'd feel better if you didn't have the weight of failure on your shoulders if we mess this up."

"Let's go over the plan one more time." Angelina suggested.

"Alright. I'm only doing this once, so listen up. I'm going to go in there, convince my double that he doesn't need to be at the party. Meanwhile, you're going to wait out here for me. If all goes well, then I'll have the sedan and we'll be riding to the party in record time.

"Now, my plan is for you to stay in the car the entire time, and then we'll make our getaway later. I'll arrive in there, ask to speak to Rain privately, lock her up in the bathroom, hands tied, and leave. Then I'll call the Huntsville Psychiatric Hospital, and they'll pick her up."

"What if they don't arrive fast enough?" Angelina asked.

"Good point. Why don't you call them now, and I'll get started to my apartment."

"Will do." Angelina gave a mock salute. "Good luck."

"Thanks. I'll need it. Though I'd prefer if you'd pray for me instead."

"Okay. See you later then."

In a matter of minutes, Joshua had made his way up the flight of stairs to his apartment. He knocked on the door, and heard his own voice calling out, "Coming!"

Joshua shivered. This was all too surreal. And spooky.

When past Joshua opened the door, he immediately gasped in surprise. "Wha-?" he sputtered.

"Just invite me inside," Joshua mumbled.

Past Joshua, still speechless, began scratching his head. "Hey, I remember you. You visited me before when we were trying to save Lapis, right? We need to save someone else?"

Joshua nodded. "Rain, and my plan requires that you stay here while you let me borrow the car. Got it?" He swiped the keys off the kitchen counter.

"Hey, wait, I want to come too. What happens to Rain?" past Joshua asked.

Joshua muttered a hurried reply. "Bob's dead, and Rain kills herself."

Past Joshua gasped. "*What?!* When? How? Why?"

"No time," Joshua said. "Just stay here, and I'll be back with the car."

Past Joshua crossed his arms. "All right, just make sure Rain is safe. And maybe go back in time and save Bob, too."

"Already tried that. Didn't work."

As Joshua hurried out the door, he heard himself call over his shoulder. "Maybe the past can't be changed. You ever think of that? You still believe in God, right? Maybe He ordered everything here to be just the way He wanted it."

Joshua knew only too well. He just hoped he wasn't too late.

Angelina was standing by his car when Joshua arrived. "Everything work out okay?" she asked.

Joshua grunted in reply. He started the engine, and soon they were off to Heidi's party.

"You call the hospital?" Joshua asked.

"Sure did. All's well." Angelina affirmed.

"Good. Now let's save Rain."

When they arrived at the Hawkins' residence, Joshua gave one last command to Angelina. "Stay here," he admonished. "Don't leave the car, please." He added on the last for politeness.

Angelina nodded her head. "Fine." She spoke. "Just save Rain, please. For Heidi's sake."

"I'll do my best." Joshua gritted his teeth as he walked into the house. He immediately saw Rain on the couch, crying her eyes out with baby Isabelle in her arms. Heidi sat close by.

Joshua immediately approached Rain. "Could I speak to you for a moment?" he asked.

Rain wiped her nose on a tissue, and sat up, handing Isabelle to Heidi. "Sure," she spoke. "Let's go into the kitchen."

Joshua grimaced within himself. Well, at least the kitchen had a bathroom off it.

Joshua decided to approach this subject the easy way and use the locking up in the bathroom thing as a last resort.

"I know what you want to do." He said it simply, with barely any inflection.

Rain stood speechless for a moment, and then a hard glint shone in her eyes. "It's not like you can stop me." She whispered stubbornly, crossing her arms in the process.

Joshua heard the sound of sirens close by, and he turned back to Rain. "I've called emergency personnel to help you. You'll stay at the psychiatric hospital for a while. Then, when you're well, you can come back home and take care of the children."

Rain noticed that Joshua was holding her wrists tightly, and she gave a shocked impression.

"No, you can't do that." She heard a knocking at the door and made an attempt to free her hands from Joshua's grip.

Somehow, she managed to slip away, and ran directly

to the knife drawer. "Emergency!" Joshau yelled. "In here!"

He struggled to restrain Rain once more, but she was

fighting ferociously, and she now had a knife in her hand.

Joshua struggled to grab the knife out of her hand, and in the meantime, she jabbed him with it in several places.

Finally, the knife found its mark, and Rain crumpled to the floor. Emergency personnel arrived, and she was declared dead on the scene.

As the EMS workers were taking care of Joshua's wounds, he realized that he had failed. Again.

Maybe his past self was right. Maybe the past couldn't be changed.

Now all he hoped was that Angelina had kept up her end of the bargain and managed to stay in the passenger seat of his car.

When he walked out, he was surprised to see her still sitting there, a look of hope on her face.

But that look dissipated when she saw Joshua's bleeding arms and chest. Her face crumpled, and she burst into tears as Rain's body was escorted out of the home and into the waiting ambulance.

Chapter 4

Joshua returned the sedan to his home, and together he and Angelina found their way back to her office.

Angelina was still whimpering, and Joshua felt close to tears himself.

"How could we have messed up so badly?" she asked, more to herself than anyone else.

"You mean how could *I* have messed up so badly." Joshua said mournfully. "None of this was your fault. It was all mine." He put his head down.

Angelina reached over to massage his arm. "Hey, it isn't your fault. You did your best, and this was the outcome."

"Yeah, failure. Just like with Lapis and with Bob."

"You can't keep blaming yourself for what happened. Maybe the past can't be changed. Maybe we should quit while we're ahead."

"No, no I can't do that. If I can't save anyone else, I must save Ellyn."

At this declaration, Angelina burst into tears. "Oh, Ellyn," she moaned. "Could you really bring her back? I miss her so much."

"Yeah. And I can save Vanessa too."

Vanessa. His bloodthirsty cousin who had killed Ellyn because of her jealous nature.

It was all rather a twisted story, but Joshua couldn't allow himself to forget it. He never saw Ellyn after she was taken away, but he could imagine the terrible scene.

Ellyn, begging for her life, while Vanessa stood over her, gun in hand. It must have been awful.

He sighed, remembering Vanessa's suicide note. She had apologized for killing Ellyn, then drowned herself in the river nearby Ellyn's house.

That letter haunted Joshua to this day.

Angelina brought him out of his reverie. "How in the world are we going to save them?"

"Not 'we.' Just me. I have to do this alone."

"But why? I can help, I know I can." Angelina whined.

"No!" Joshua said, a little bit too loudly. "No," he said more quietly. "It's not necessary. I have a lot of thinking to do, but you can't come. I can't risk something happening to you so you wouldn't be able to come back home. Your husband would never forgive me. Or believe me."

Angelina laughed uncomfortably. "All right. You have me convinced." She sobered. "Just let me know if you need something, okay? I'm always here to help."

Joshua nodded his assent. "Of course."

He looked into Amber's eyes. "He was carrying a watch with him, eh?" he said.

"Yes sir, Mr. Fritz, and I do believe he knew about your plan. He said it was a grave emergency."

"Hmmm" Fritz thought to himself. "We need to get ahold of that watch. Think you can do that?"

"Of course, Mr. Fritz, sir."

"Good. See to it that you do. I'd like to take a look at that little clock piece. And you're sure what Emmy said is true?"

"Yes, sir. She said the woman was rubbing the watch, and they held hands, and they disappeared."

"I see. Well, make sure you find it. This could be the answer to many world problems. Unless your friend is lying."

"Oh, no. She wouldn't do that."

Just like the night before, Joshua barely got any sleep. He kept thinking about what his past self had said. About the fact that you couldn't change the past. It was a depressing thought, but Joshua resolved that he would at least see Ellyn one last time.

He didn't really have a plan. He wanted Andrew Mitchell, Ellyn's former husband, out of the picture.

He knew a good deal about Ellyn's history, as her and her friends had been very forthcoming about the details.

So, Joshua knew when Andrew and Ellyn had first met. Ellyn had been taking her younger sister, Lizzy, to a children's home in Pennsylvania, and Andrew had been watching in the downpour as the two sisters waited on the doorstep.

As Joshua remembered it, Andrew had been watching from a tree, so if he could somehow get him to come down, tackle him maybe...

But not kill him. Joshua would never do that.

Just ensure that Andrew and Ellyn never met. Maybe pay him off to stay away from her.

Yeah, like he had any money. He didn't even have a job, having gotten fired two weeks ago.

So, he would do that.

It wasn't a great plan, but it would ensure that Ellyn wouldn't have to deal with his abuse for the rest of her life.

He'd give her a good life, and she would never have to die.

But first, he'd have to deal with Vanessa.

He had to make sure she was never transferred to the Huntsville Psychiatric Hospital.

That way, she would never meet Ellyn, and have no reason to be jealous.

Or better yet, go farther back into the past and persuade his past self to spend more time caring for his ward. Then maybe he could introduce himself to Ellyn, and they could get things started on the right foot. Not like the first time.

Joshua smiled. He remembered when they had first met. It seemed like only yesterday...

He had just finished signing the paperwork that established Vanessa as a patient at Huntsville Psychiatric. He was holding one of those gross hospital coffees in his hand that Huntsville was known for, and he didn't see the pretty blonde heading directly for Vanessa's room.

She had her gaze down, looking at a clipboard she held in her hands.

Neither of them was looking where they were going, and they both looked up at the same time.

Not fast enough however, for they both rammed into each other, Joshua's coffee going everywhere. Literally, all over her attire.

Joshua was amazed that she didn't scream when the boiling hot liquid ran down her face and into her eyes. He couldn't stop apologizing.

"I am so, so sorry." He said over and over.

"It's fine," she said, altogether flustered. That was the first time he had seen her eyes. They were beautiful. Azure, with a hint of lavender. He found himself staring at her, much longer than necessary.

"Uh," she said. "Could you get me a paper towel?" she asked.

"Oh, uh, right." He went back into Vanessa's room and came out with a box of tissues. "Kleenex okay?" he grinned.

She grinned back. "Definitely not funny, but okay."

"So, uh," Joshua mumbled. "Can I take you out for coffee? You're really pretty." He blushed profusely, startled at his own boldness.

Ellyn smiled. "Kind of shallow, don't you think, just to date a woman because she's pretty." She laughed. "But I'll take it. However, maybe we should just go with tea, or something." She had laughed again.

Joshua closed his recollection. That was nearly twenty-five years ago. Life had been so easy back then. When had it ever gotten so difficult?

When Ellyn died, leaving him just as Lapis had. He had never claimed his life was easy, but he seemed to have more struggles than the average person.

It was depressing, really. That the two women he most loved in the world were gone. But he would change that.

Maybe Lapis was truly gone forever, but there was still a chance he could save Ellyn. A small chance, but a chance, nonetheless.

So, his plan.

Go back to the children's home when Ellyn and Lizzy, her sister, first arrived. Next, stop Andrew from ever meeting Ellyn.

And, if they did marry, keep Andrew from hurting Ellyn. Joshua wasn't sure how he was going to do that, but he wasn't about to give up.

After that, he would tell his former self to spend more time taking care of Vanessa. Keep her away from all psychiatric hospitals, and make sure she loved Ellyn when he met her.

Then, he could marry Ellyn, and the three would live together, at least until Vanessa was ready to leave home. The girl was twenty-three when she died; Joshua hoped he could get Vanessa stable enough to live on her own, and then he would have Ellyn all to himself.

Well, excluding her friends and family, job, and God.

He would have to get God back into his life at some point. But right now, that just wasn't happening.

So, he had his plan all laid out. Get in, get out, get back to spend the perfect life with his aging Ellyn. Nothing could possibly go wrong.

He rubbed the watch and imagined where he wanted to be. As he disappeared from view, he was unaware of two women watching him from the window on the porch that surrounded the apartment building complex. Emmy and Amber. They needed that watch. And they were going to get it.

The world spun for a moment or two. Then Joshua covered his eyes as a torrential downpour of rain fell upon him.

He glimpsed the silhouette of two girls standing at the entrance of the children's home, a stately building that had now become a rundown mansion.

For a moment, Joshua wondered if the place was still standing, years later, but then reminded himself to focus.

He looked up into a copse of trees, only a few feet from where Ellyn and Lizzy stood, and he saw Andrew sitting, watching, a menacing gleam in his harsh eyes.

Joshua stealthily walked over. "Hey, kid! Andrew! Come down here for a second!" he called as loud as he could.

Andrew, visibly startled, immediately made his way down from the trees.

"Sir," he said. He was startled, Joshua could tell. And looked like a rabbit about to bound away in search of shelter.

He couldn't let that happen.

"Look kid, I want you to stay away from her, you hear me?" Joshua used his most intimidating voice.

Andrew looked Joshua up and down. "What's it to you? You her old man, or something?"

Joshua smiled grimly. "Just think of me as her guardian. "Now I know all about your little games, about that girl that killed herself here, and how you covered it up."

Andrew looked extremely alarmed, maybe even a little disturbed. "How would you know that?" he asked wearily.

"Don't ask questions. Just do as I say. Or your little secret's going to come out."

Andrew suddenly smiled sardonically. "What'd you say her name was?" he asked.

Joshua gave him a hard stare. "Ellyn." He said simply. But immediately regretted it when Andrew immediately called out.

"Ellyn, over here, Ellyn!"

The skinny runt of a girl looked over at him in a frightened sort of way. She walked back into the rain, and raced towards them, like a cat with its fur ruffled. "How did you know my name?" she asked critically, studying the two figures before her. "Do you know my father? Well, you can take me, but I won't have you taking Lizzy."

Andrew spoke up. "Well, I don't know anything about your dad, but I'll bet this old man does." He hoisted a finger at Joshua. "I'll see you later, Ellyn." He flashed Ellyn a brilliant smile and trotted away, as though he didn't have a care in the world.

Ellyn looked at Joshua harshly. "You know my father? Richard Lyss. You're working for him, aren't you?" Ellyn put her hands on her hips.

"No, of course not, I..." Joshua's voice trailed off as he noticed the early beauty of this young girl.

"Then who are you?" Ellyn interjected in his thoughts.

"I'm sorry," Joshua said. "I can't tell you my real name. It would mess up everything. But look, I'm a friend, okay? I care about you. I don't want to see you come to harm. All right?"

Ellyn looked at him, terrified. Then he realized what she was looking at. Him. Joshua Reynolds. A sixty-one-year-old man, who sounded like a child predator.

Joshua slapped a hand across his forehead. "Man, I'm such an idiot." He muttered to himself. "Look, Ellyn, I'm sorry—"

"You never did tell me how you knew my name." Ellyn looked at him as if he were a wolf, about to bite down on her. She stopped his answer. "Look, I have to go. My sister is waiting for me." She began backing away from Joshua, slowly, as if afraid he might attack her.

"I would never hurt you." He said. "I love you."

But she would never hear the words. She was already going back to the front door, and he could see her tiny fist knocking. Her little sister, Lizzy, grasped her older sister as tightly as she could, and even from here, Joshua could see the bond between the two. It was touching, really.

Joshua felt for the watch and pulled it out of his pocket. He caressed it softly, and imagined himself back at his apartment, which wouldn't be his for very much longer...

Chapter 5

When Joshua woke up the next morning, he couldn't get Ellyn out of his mind.

He knew he was doomed to fail her as well, but after seeing her as a young girl, his want to see her as a grown woman once again grew.

It wasn't a romantic attraction; no, he simply wanted to see her again for what she was. A kind-hearted, sweet person.

There weren't many of those left in his world.

Joshua looked at the watch sitting on his bedside table.

He promptly turned over and rolled onto his other side, out of view of the watch. A great knocking jerked him awake again, and he slowly climbed out of bed.

"Coming!" he called, but much to his annoyance, the knocking persisted, only harder this time.

For some reason, Joshua felt an intense need to grab the watch and take it with him to the door. As he shuffled to the entrance, he shoved the watch into his shirt pocket.

As he opened the door, he was suddenly confronted with the faces of two women he oddly recognized.

Ah yes. Amber from the bank, and Emmy from the hospital.

Amber put on a sunny disposition. "Hello, Mr. Reynolds, sir." She said politely.

He gave a half smile, laced with grimness. "And how are you, ladies?" It wasn't much of a question.

The tenseness in the air was tangible. They each looked at each other awkwardly for a few moments, until Emmy noticed the round bulge in Joshua's pocket.

She made a lunge for it and he slammed the door in her face.

However, he didn't lock it, and she easily made her way inside.

"What do you want?" Joshua hollered.

"Obviously." Emmy rolled her eyes. "The watch, silly."

Amber made a grab for it, but failed. Things were getting out of hand, and finally Joshua removed it from his pocket and began rubbing it furiously.

He imagined where he wanted to go, and the room began to spin. But the two women were clinging to him fiercely, and Joshua understood that this wasn't escape from his problem. He was only getting into a bigger one.

When Joshua arrived at the front of Ellyn's home, the two women were still grasping him tightly.

This was the year 1994, just three years before Ellyn would be killed, but only a few months before Vanessa would enter her first psychiatric hospital at the age of twenty.

Joshua flung the women off him and raced towards the front door of Ellyn's house.

He knew he would be a stranger to her, but hopefully that wouldn't deter her from allowing him into her house.

If she was even home.

He rang the doorbell three times consecutively and was full of relief when the door opened, and Ellyn appeared.

Without waiting for an introduction, Joshua burst into the house and slammed the door behind him, locking it in the process.

He was out of breath, and he wasn't surprised to see Ellyn looking at him quizzically.

"Excuse me, sir," she said haltingly. "But do I know you?" She gave a casual smile, initiating that she wasn't afraid of this old man in her house.

Joshua gathered his bearings. "No, uh. You don't. I mean, I know you, but you don't know me."

His voice trailed off, as he dug in his pocket for the watch.

It wasn't there.

Panicked, Joshua searched all his pockets, but to no avail. The watch was gone.

And so were the women.

Joshua slapped his hand against his forehead. "I'm such an idiot!" he exclaimed.

Ellyn, now even more confused, gave him a curious look.

"Why don't you start by telling me your name." she said.

"Who, me? Oh, right. I'm Joshua Reynolds." He wondered if giving his name would ruin everything.

"And what seems to be your predicament?" Ellyn asked in the calm soothing voice that she was known for.

"Well, I'm stuck here." Joshua began.

"Oh, no, you're not. I have a truck, and I'd be happy to take you wherever you need to go. So, you can cross that problem off your list." She smiled up at him brilliantly.

"No, you don't understand, Ellyn. I'm stuck here. I'm from the future. I came to warn you, and...change things. But those women, they took my watch, and now I'm stuck in the past, here, forever." All of this came out in a tumult of words, and Joshua was surprised to see that Ellyn wasn't even looking at him strangely.

"I see. How about we start with: how do you know my name?"

"Your name? Well, we'll meet in the future, and I'll spill coffee all over you. We're at the hospital, and I'm just securing Vanessa in the facility. You know, making sure she's all right, and stuff."

"Who's Vanessa?" Ellyn probed.

"My cousin. She has, uh, real mental health issues. She, uh, she kills you in the future."

Ellyn couldn't help emitting a little gasp.

"Yeah, that's why I'm here." Joshua continued. "I'm here to save you. I wanted to make sure to tell my past self not to let Vanessa stay at Huntsville Psychiatric. To spend more time with her. That kind of thing."

Ellyn couldn't get over the killing part. "Your cousin...kills me?" she said. "I'll be murdered? What happens to Rain?"

Joshua wondered how much he should say. Finally, he decided to divulge all of it. "Rain marries a wonderful man named Bob, but a few days ago, in my time, he gets murdered himself."

"What?! How? Why?"

"He was in some debt. A lot of it. Mr. Fritz, that's the banker, planned a hijacking that killed Bob in his car."

"How did Rain take that? Please tell my baby girl didn't—"

At Joshua's ashen look, Ellyn burst into tears. "I went back into the past." Joshua said. "I tried to save her, and Bob too." He was about to say, "And Lapis," but refrained. "But I failed. I'm so sorry."

Ellyn let herself fall into his arms, sobbing as she did so. "What's wrong with my family? My whole family is crazy!" she exclaimed.

Joshua thought of all he knew of her family history, and he couldn't help but agree. However, he didn't say anything.

He just continued to hold her. At least that felt right.

Amber and Emmy stared at the watch. "How do you think it works?" Emmy asked.

Amber shrugged. "Dunno. I saw him rubbing it. Maybe that has something to do with it."

"Mr. Fritz is going to be angry if we don't get this back to him on time."

"What does he want with it anyway? I mean, the little gadget's kind of cool, but why would he want to go back to the past? Unless something terrible happened and he's trying to fix it."

"Stop pretending like you know anything." Emmy said. "I don't know any more than you do, so stop thinking you know so much. Because you don't. Now help me figure it out."

"All right, all right." Amber admonished. She took the watch in her fingers and studied it carefully. "Maybe we just imagine where we want to go, and boom, we're there."

"I don't think that's right. But I guess we could give it a try."

"Okay. Let's hold hands. I think that's how we'll stay connected."

"Sure, sure." Emmy said. She grasped Amber's hand. "We have the key to time itself, so, where do you want to go?"

"Right to Mr. Fritz office, that's where. And don't you get any pretty ideas in your head, Emmy. I don't want anything to do with this device."

Together, the two held hands, and they both imagined themselves back in Mr. Fritz office.

Suddenly, they were there, and each gave a cry of joy. "Back to the present!" Amber crowed, and Emmy joined in.

Mr. Fritz' office chair turned, and soon he was standing there before them. "Why, hello girls." He smiled, and a dark glint covered his eyes. "Did you bring what I requested?"

"Oh yes sir," they said in unison. Amber handed him the watch.

Mr. Fritz examined it closely, caressing it as he did so. "Finally, the power to go back in time, fix something that never should have happened."

At his vague remark, the girls turned to look at each other, and finally Mr. Fritz dismissed them.

When he was alone, he pulled a photograph out of his desk drawer. On it, was an image of him, with his son-in-law, Joshua Reynolds, and his beloved daughter, Lapis.

He turned over the image and found the note that was inscribed there. "Dear Mr. Lazuli," it said, for indeed, that was his real name. "Hope you have a great summer. Best regards, Josh."

"So, my friend. You are now lost in time forever." He murmured to himself. "Well, we'll fix that. Just wait until I get my hands on you."

He rubbed the watch, thought of all he was going to do to Joshua, wherever he was, and instantly vanished.

As Ellyn's sobbing dissipated, Joshua released his tight hold on her. "Sorry," he mumbled.

"No, no, it's okay." Ellyn said. She wrapped her arms around herself and squeezed, seeming to pull herself back together.

She sniffed. "Okay, so what do we do?"

"You're not doing anything," a voice snarled, and they both turned to see a man walking towards them.

They both spoke at the same time.

"Mr. Fritz?"

"Mr. Lazuli?"

The two stared at each other in bewilderment. "Wait how do you know him?" Joshua asked. Fritz sounded so familiar. Where had he so recently heard that name?

"Mr. Fritz is my banker." Ellyn said. She seemed to notice him for the first time. "Wait, what's happened to you? You look so different..." she trailed off, not wanting to state the obvious that Mr. Fritz once beanpole frame was now heavily overweight.

Joshua interjected. "Wait, I know who you are now. Mr. Fritz, the one who got Bob Hawkins killed because he owed too much money. But I know you as Mr. Lazuli, the father of my late wife..." he seemed at a loss for words. Suddenly Joshua noticed the watch clasped in Mr. Fritz/Lazuli's fist.

"Hey, that's my watch!" he exclaimed. "You had your henchmen steal it from me!"

The man tsked. "No, no, no, no. I always intended to give it back. Just as soon as I saved Lapis from your father."

Ellyn looked thoroughly confused. "Wait, what is going on? And what should I really call you, Mr. Fritz?"

"Frank is fine. At least that name is real." He shrugged.

Joshua was still a bit befuddled. "Why did you change your name?"

Frank didn't seem loathe to leave out any details. A bad sign. Especially with the silhouette of a gun in Frank's pocket of his pants.

"Oh, I killed my wife. That's all. I had to go undercover."

Ellyn gasped.

"Why?" Joshua demanded, on the verge of tears himself. Mrs. Lazuli had been like a mother to him.

"I couldn't take it anymore. All the weeping and crying. Day and night, all the time. No man could bear to see his wife in such pain, so I put her out of her misery."

"A mercy killing," Ellyn whispered, aghast.

Joshua crossed his arms. "So why are you here now?" he asked Frank.

"Because." Frank gave a sinister smile. "I need your help."

"Like I'd ever help you." Joshua said. "You're a murderer!" he shouted.

Suddenly Frank grabbed the gun out of his pocket. "Looks like you don't have a choice." He smiled. "Help me, or you die, and I pin it on your girlfriend."

"No one would ever believe you." Ellyn said. "I'd tell them the truth. You'd never get away with it."

"Or perhaps I would." In one quick flash, Joshua was on the ground, writhing in pain at the shot in his arm.

Ellyn screamed. "You tried to kill him!" she cried.

"Oh, no, my dear girl. Not kill him. Get him to wake up to what's right and come with me."

"Nothing you're doing is right." Ellyn said furiously.

"Get him up, would you? He's always been a crybaby."

"What are you going to do?"

"I'm going to go back in time, my dear. To save my precious little girl from the likes of inhumane beings like Jim Reynolds."

"What happened?"

"There was a fire. Lapis went in to get her Bible, and she never came back out." Frank seemed to tear up at the slightest insinuation of his daughter.

"So, what's your plan?" Ellyn asked defensively.

"What's the use in not telling you? You're just going to die anyway. Very well. I'm sending Joshua in to rescue Lapis. Hopefully, and if my calculations are correct, she'll come back out, and he won't."

Joshua groaned from the floor. "Frank," he moaned, his voice barely above a whisper, "I already tried to save Lapis. When I first found the watch, our old home was the first place I went."

He continued. "You can't change the past, Frank. I realize that now. God destined Lapis to die that day, just like He destined Bob to die under your hand. It's just the way God ordered the world when He gave us freewill."

Frank laughed emotionlessly. "Don't you see? I don't care what you say. You're part of my plan, and nothing can stop me, not even God." He held the watch up with his hand. "With this device, I can control time. I am God!" He looked triumphantly at the ceiling, as if daring God to intervene.

"You're wrong." Joshua slowly stood at his feet. He made eye contact with Ellyn, and they seemed to be thinking the same thing. Together they lunged for the watch.

Even though they missed, they did manage to catch Frank off guard. He lost his footing and fell to the ground.

Ellyn fell down as well, and she grabbed the watch out of Frank's hand, tossing it to Joshua's good arm. "Take it!" She yelled, not unnecessarily. Frank was breathing very loudly.

"Take it," she repeated. "And get some medical attention for your arm. I'll give Frank here a sedative, and he should be sleeping soundly soon."

Joshua hesitated to go. "I don't want to leave you here. Alone, with him."

She looked up at him, her beautiful blond hair falling into her face. She smiled. "Don't worry about me. He's incapacitated right now. But he won't be for long." She looked at him. "Looks like he's suffered a minor heart attack. I'll call an ambulance, and everything will be fine. Go on," she encouraged.

"Okay," Joshua said doubtfully. He imagined himself back at his apartment in the present day, then suddenly changed his mind. There was someone he needed to speak to first.

Angelina listened to his story with interest. And a little bit of concern. "So, you saw Ellyn?" she asked finally. "How was she? Did she look okay? Did you see Rain?"

Joshua answered all her questions. "Ellyn looked great. A little thin, maybe, but overall good. I didn't see Rain, but I can only assume she was sleeping in one of the back rooms."

"And that man you saw was there, Frank, also known as Mr. Fritz, also known as Mr. Lazuli. Am I right so far?" At Joshua's nod, she continued. "So, this guy, who actually killed Bob, or at least had it done, also happens to be your father-in-law, is that right?"

She looked at him from over her glasses. Joshua nodded again, and he was reminded of the day when this very same woman had interrogated him for the murder of Ellyn Lyss.

His Ellyn.

Who probably right now was waiting in the hospital for some guy she barely even knew, just so she could talk to him.

Because Ellyn was like that. A sweet, kind-hearted person.

He wondered what she was doing at that moment...

Ellyn waited in the lobby. She was cold, and the unfamiliar surroundings frightened her. She couldn't help thinking about how similar this hospital was to her own.

The thought comforted her somewhat, but anyone who knew Ellyn knew she didn't like going to new places.

After a car accident she had endured years ago, before Rain was even born, she had had a wary fear of hospitals, which was somewhat ironic considering the fact that she worked in one and had been doing so for many years.

So, here she waited. For what, she wasn't sure. Just that she needed to be there. For this man, who had nobody.

A few hours later they had Frank stabilized, and he was allowed visitors.

Ellyn walked in tentatively, noticing a monitor, sometimes called a sitter, sitting in the corner of the room.

"Do you mind if we speak alone?" she asked the monitor politely.

The woman huffed. "No can do, missy," she said a little too loudly. "This man here's on suicide watch. He's been talking some craziness about time travel, and we're trying to get him calmed down."

Ellyn walked over to Frank's bedside, and placed a small hand on one of his own. "Frank, it's me, Ellyn." She whispered softly, not wishing to disturb him if he was sleeping soundly.

Frank stirred slightly, and his eyes opened. A look of shock replaced his languid appearance in an instant, and he was on his guard. "What do you want? Why are you here?" he growled at her.

She smiled sweetly, lowering her voice so the monitor couldn't hear, even though she could see her struggling to make out what they were saying. "Joshua's coming back, after he gets fixed up." She promised him.

"Why in the world would I trust him?" Frank muttered loudly.

"Shh, keep your voice down." She quieted him. "The only reason he didn't take you then was because you had suffered a mild heart attack, and Joshua was in a lot of pain. Because *you* shot him." She fixed him with a pointed glare.

"What was I supposed to do? You're given one chance to save your daughter's life, and he wasn't going to help me. I needed some leverage. Give me a break."

"No, I'm not going to do that. Because you shot him. And didn't you hear what he said. He tried to save Lapis before he tried to save me and that Bob Hawkins guy. Lapis was first on his to-do list. Don't you get that?"

"Fine. But maybe he didn't try hard enough. I'm sure I could do better than he could."

"No, I'm not sure you can. I don't know all the details, but I'm sure there was nothing he could do. It was his *wife*. Don't you think he would try to save her, of all people?

"So why are saying all this? What's your point?"

Ellyn had a keen memory. "My point is, forgive Joshua's dad. I don't know the reason any of this happened, but you must forgive. What do you think Jesus would have done? Held a grudge, and killed people who didn't think His way? I don't think so."

"I guess not." Frank grumbled.

"Do you want to pray with me?"

"What for?"

"Why, to accept Jesus into your heart. I know you can feel Him calling for you."

Together, the two prayed.

And Frank accepted Christ as his Savior.

Chapter 6

Angelina continued her narrative.

"So, this guy, who wanted Bob dead over a matter of money, also killed his wife because he 'wanted to put her out of her misery.' Okay, and now he wants to bring his daughter back, because she died in a fire.

"Answer me this then. How in the world is he going to explain away the whole mother situation? I mean, it's not like she just got up and disappeared. Right? Think about that."

"I'm guessing he didn't think that far. However, now we know that we can't change the past, that pulls a whole other spin on things."

Joshua briefly went back to his conversation with that old homeless man who had given him the watch in the first place. He had wondered then why the man hadn't gotten rid of it. He could kind of understand now.

"You can't change the past," he murmured to himself, and Angelina looked up from the notes she had been taking.

"What's that you said?" she looked up.

"Oh, nothing," Joshua mumbled and returned to the topic at hand.

Suddenly Angelina gave a screech. "Your arm, your arm!" she shouted. "What happened? Did you get shot?"

Joshua nodded his head, suddenly aware of the pain that had had a numbing effect before. He had wrapped a makeshift bandage around the area, but now a large amount of blood was seeping through.

"We need to get you to a hospital!" Angelina exclaimed. "Is this why you came back without Frank? For assistance?"

"No. Frank had a heart attack." Now that awareness had been brought to his wound, he suddenly felt nauseous. "I think I'm going to lay down now." He slumped to the floor, and Angelina screamed for help.

Joshua woke up, dazed, and in a hospital bed.

"What?" he mumbled to himself, before feeling the stabbing pain in his arm. He gritted his teeth and clicked the call button.

And who should appear before him but that odd nurse, Emmy.

She smiled at him sweetly, and Joshua noticed the camera in the right-hand corner of the room.

"And how is our patient doing today?" she asked.

Joshua realized it was morning. He decided to be cordial. "How long was I out?" he asked, scratching his head.

Emmy glanced at her watch. "Well, you slept soundly through last afternoon, and last night, as well, so I'd say fifteen hours, maybe? Don't quote me on that. Why?"

"Just asking." Joshua noticed the demeanor of the nurse. Sure, she was flighty, but today, she seemed different.

Not that he knew her well, but he was good at reading people.

Like there was something she wanted to tell him but couldn't quite get the words out.

She sat down on the bed beside him. "Mr. Fritz told me everything, you know. I don't know where he is now. But he told me about his daughter. His real name is Lazuli, isn't it?"

Joshua wasn't sure what to say. "Yeah, why?"

"Oh, it's just that I grew up in Florida. A little town in the Sunshine state. Amber and I both did. It's not too much of a coincidence that I grew up with Lapis while she was living there. Or is it?"

Maybe the nurse was crazy.

"Maybe it's too much of a coincidence that when I came of age, I followed her here, only to find her dead.

They say it was the husband's fault, and I guess that would be you. So, tell me. How did my best friend die?"

Joshua gulped inwardly. "I didn't kill her." He managed. Joshua wondered how much Lazuli had told her.

"It was a fire, and" he still got choked up, "I couldn't save her."

Emmy delivered a full-on slap to his face. "Do you know how much she meant to me? How much she meant to Amber? And you took her away!"

"No, I didn't. The entire Lazuli family moved. It's not my fault, and if you want someone to blame, blame Frank."

"Frank? Who on earth is Frank?"

"Frank Lazuli? Frank Fritz? Come on, Emmy, think."

"Don't you get familiar with me! This is all your fault, you know."

Joshua grasped her arm, wincing as he did so. "Hey, let go of me!"

He wrestled her down. "Now, just listen to me. This wasn't my fault. This wasn't your fault. Lapis is gone now, and nothing is bringing her back."

"But the watch. The watch will bring her back."

"No, it won't. I already tried. The past is stuck in the past, and it can't alter the future."

"You're lying!" Emmy shouted. "You're a filthy dirty, liar! As soon as I find that watch, I'll save Lapis, you'll see!"

Suddenly Emmy's gaze turned cynical. "And with Lapis by my side, I'll take away everything you ever loved. I'll destroy your life."

Joshua's blood ran cold. "You're not, you're not."

Emmy laughed hysterically. "Gay? No, I'm not. I just believe in a little thing called friendship. And when Lapis realizes you didn't save her, she'll take my side, and together we'll burn down everything you've ever loved, brick by brick."

"You won't get away with this."

"I'm afraid I already have." She pulled away from his grip and walked towards the door. "I'm having you committed. To Huntsville Psychiatric. For insisting you can travel back in time." She laughed. "How ironic. And they'll never let you keep your watch. It's as good as mine.

"Why would they give it to you?"

She smiled. "Because I told them I'm the only family you have left. All your possessions will go to me."

She left the room. And Joshua had never felt so alone.

Until he remembered the watch. He needed to get out of here soon, and fast. He had hidden the watch in an unknown pocket on the inside of his jacket.

The jacket in question was lying beside his bed, wrapped around a chair. He reached for it, swiping at it, and missing it.

He quickly looked up at the small observation window to see if anyone noticed. He let out a quick exhale of breath when someone didn't come in and try to stop him.

He lunged for the jacket again. This time he got it, but not without half falling out of the bed.

"I'm too old for this." He grumbled to himself, before crawling back to the center of the bed.

He rubbed the watch between his two hands and imagined where he wanted to be-a hospital room where he hoped both Frank and Ellyn were located.

At that moment, doctors came pouring into the room, and Joshua rubbed the watch faster.

Emmy was at the head of the procession. Her eyes narrowed. "Get that watch out of his hands!" she shouted, seemingly in charge.

But it was too late. Once again, Joshua had vanished without a trace.

Emmy attempted to hold in her feelings, but she screamed instead. "You let him get away!" she hollered. "Ugh!" and she fell into a sloppy puddle on the ground.

As it turned out, Ellyn and Frank were actually in the lobby when Joshua arrived. Frank held a huge smile on his face, and he clasped Ellyn's small hand in his own. She too, was smiling.

Joshua looked at them both up and down. "I feel like I've missed something. Would someone care to enlighten me?"

"Oh, yes," Ellyn enthused. "Frank here just got saved. We were on our way out of the hospital, as he just got discharged, as well." She turned to Frank. "I'm sure you're ready to be back home."

Joshua thought of Frank's two adjutants, Amber, and Emmy, and how Emmy had promised a certain destruction of everything Joshua loved. He shivered. He would have to have a talk with Frank about that, if he was truly different.

"It will be good to be back." Frank rubbed his hands together. "There's going to be some changes at my bank from now on."

He suddenly turned soberly on Joshua. "Hey, I'm sorry about your friend, okay? He posed a threat to my financial gain, but I didn't handle things well. I'm truly sorry."

Joshua shrugged him off. "Don't apologize to me. Apologize to the wife who killed herself because her husband was dead."

Frank looked mortified, and he stared around the busy hospital lobby. "Maybe we should take this outside," he suggested.

"Agreed." Joshua said coolly, and together all three walked to the outdoor area. Joshua grasped the watch firmly in his hand.

Ellyn walked with her hands in her pockets, as if feigning cold. All three of them sat down on a long park bench nearby.

"Again, I'm really sorry about your friend." Frank said morosely.

"It's okay, really it is. Bob's is a better place now, and that's all that matters."

"I hope I can make it up to you someday."

"Let's start in our own time zone." He turned towards Ellyn. "Elly," he said, using her pet name. "I'm really going to miss you."

"I barely even know you, yet somehow I feel like we've known each other forever." Ellyn said.

Joshua hoped that was a compliment. "Look, I, uh. A lot's going to happen to you in the future, but I don't want you to live in fear."

Ellyn smiled. "I won't," she whispered.

Joshua had one final message. He grinned as he said it. "And, uh, when you see the young me for the first-time spilling coffee all over you, don't let on that you already knew about me."

Ellyn smiled again. "I won't," she promised.

"Look, I know I can't stop Vanessa from hurting you," he whispered, out of the earshot of Frank, "But could you please still be kind to her, for my sake?"

"Of course." Ellyn agreed. She looked over at Frank. "I think he's getting antsy. You'd better go."

"Right, so uh." Joshua held out his hand for her to shake.

Ellyn rolled her eyes, grabbed him in a hug, and gave him a slight peck on the cheek. "This must look so weird to passerby," she whispered in his ear. "You're old enough to be my dad."

"I know, I know." Joshua held her close, not wanting this moment to ever come to an end.

But, in short order, it did. And as Ellyn walked away, smiling over her shoulder, Joshua thought of how much he was going to miss her.

She was going to die one day, yet she wasn't afraid, because she was ready to meet her Maker, her Savior, Jesus.

Joshua returned to Frank. "You ready for this?" he smiled, picturing himself at the bank where Frank worked.

"Always." The two grasped hands, and the world began to spin.

Suddenly they found themselves in Frank's office.

"Well, this is goodbye." Joshua said.

"For now, anyway. I hope to see you again. And tell your friends I'm sorry for what happened to Bob. Really, I am. Tell them that."

"Will do. And Frank, if you need anything, I'm just a call away."

"I'll remember that." Frank smiled, and Joshua began the slow walk to his home. It wouldn't be long before he was out on the streets. Maybe Frank would loan him some money.

Then again, he didn't want to be in debt to that man, even if he was a Christian now.

Joshua needed the long walk home. It gave him time to think over everything that had happened to him.

Abruptly he noticed something out of the ordinary. It was the old man, the one who had given the watch to him.

He immediately made his way over, and a strange chill came over him. Something wasn't right.

He looked at the man slumped over some bushes, and immediately realized he was dead by the stinking odor of death lurking all around him.

"Who could have done this to you?" he whispered more to himself than anyone else, then noticed a small scrap of paper tightly held in Peter's grip.

Slowly unraveling the man's fingers from the tiny piece of paper. He read it slowly, his heart in his throat.

"More of your friends will die if you don't deliver me the watch."

The paper gave an address, and a simple initial was the only signature.

E.

So, Emmy was behind all this. Probably working in cahoots with Amber. Joshua shivered, never imagining himself in this type of situation.

And he didn't have an escape plan.

Maybe, maybe he could talk to Angelina about all this. She might have a plan.

Joshua ran the rest of the way to his apartment, went inside and grabbed his keys, then finally made his way to his car. Opening the driver's seat, he dove in and drove to Angelina's office. He was sure she would be there.

When he arrived at Angelina's office door, he was surprised to see it unlocked.

Angelina always locked her door.

Knocking softly, Joshua opened the door. He was doubly surprised to see that Angelina wasn't there.

However, he wasn't astounded to see a tiny piece of paper on Angelina's desk that was folded in half.

He grasped it with shaking hands, opening it carefully.

"If you want to see your precious friend alive, you better hand over the watch."

Again, an address was given, and the initial E was written in the bottom right corner.

Not knowing what to do, Joshua strode to the reception desk and asked to speak to a detective there.

The woman at the desk looked apologetic. "I'm sorry, sir. But Angelina Carmen was the only detective in today, and she went for a lunch break two hours ago. I'm afraid she's gone home for the day."

Joshua gritted his teeth. So, this was how Emmy was going to play it. She wasn't joking about taking away all his friends.

Suddenly Joshua had an intense desire to make sure Heidi was all right.

Before the receptionist had a chance to offer more sympathy, Joshua had raced out the door and to his car.

He drove as quickly as he could to Teresa Morgan's house, where Heidi had been staying for the past several days.

There was a scrap of paper posted on the front door.

"The only chance of you ever seeing your friends again is if you hand over the watch."

What was the big deal? He'd happily give it to her if it meant he could have his life back. He didn't want anything to do with that stupid watch.

An address was given, and Joshua plugged it into his phone. The location was ten minutes away.

Joshua wasn't familiar with that part of Huntsville, even though he'd lived here all his life.

He drove slowly, and with deliberate carefulness. He almost missed his turn into a dark alley, then drove on to a dilapidated old building.

It looked like the perfect place to keep hostages.

Joshua jumped out of the car and raced to the front door of the treacherous house. He knocked twice, tapping his foot impatiently.

Finally, he heard someone on the stairs, and saw Amber open the door. "Good," she nodded approvingly. "You've arrived. I'll let Emmy know."

She hurried away, leaving Joshua on the doorstep. However, she had left the door unlocked, and Joshua made his way inside.

He was surprised at the well-furnished décor of the place. Everything was spic and span, and the beautiful ornate rugs stood out against the beautiful hard-wood floors. On the wall were great big images of bouquets of all kinds, and a cornucopia dotted the entire left wall in a mural.

As Joshua looked about him, he was amazed at the difference between the outside and inside of the building. It was like a fantastical ancient castle in here.

Emmy sidled up next to him. "Why, hello Mr. Reynolds. So glad to see you here." She said in a sticky sweet sort of way.

It turned Joshua's stomach.

"I assume you have the watch, then?" she asked.

"Wait, I need to see my friends first." Joshua held the watch tightly in his fist.

Emmy made a grab for it, and Amber pursued him as well. Together they managed to pry the watch out of Joshua's hands.

"You don't have them!" he exclaimed.

Emmy laughed. "No, I killed them. That old man, the two women and that little girl. They're all dead."

"No!!!" Joshua lunged for Emmy, who had seemingly taken away everything he had worked to achieve. All because of a stupid watch and an oath to friendship.

As Emmy and Amber gripped hands, she made one last comment. "When I come back with Lapis with me, we'll see who she picks to love more. Her savior, me, or you, a husband who let her die."

Joshua looked up from his bereavement. "Wait, you're bringing her back here?" he asked, astonished.

"Yes. That way I'll be taking her away from young you *and* old you." She laughed, a jeering cynical laugh.

"Come on, Amber, let's go."

Amber stared at Joshua. Was that a look of pity in her gaze as she looked down upon him? He couldn't tell, and before long, they both had been whooshed away, back into the past.

Joshua wondered what he was supposed to do now. Wait for them to come back with Lapis, he supposed.

What should he do in the meantime? He had to wait here, for surely that was what they were expecting him to do.

Well, he might at least have a look around here. Maybe he would come across the bodies of his dead friends.

He most certainly hoped he would not.

Joshua wondered at that look of pity he had seen on Amber's face. Maybe he could turn her over to his side.

But perhaps not, and all was lost.

The most he could hope for was that Lapis would take his side. He wondered what it would be like to see her again.

Heartbreaking, probably.

Surely Emmy knew Lapis couldn't stay in their world. She couldn't possibly be that dense, could she?

Anything was possible in this world, Joshua thought to himself. Everything was strange.

And it had all started with that man, Peter, who had given him the watch.

But no, it hadn't really started there, it had really started with Heidi's party. Bob being killed, Rain taking her life.

Oh, everything was so complicated.

Joshua explored the massive building while he waited for the three women to arrive.

The whole house was decorated in that old gothic style, with the plush rugs and the massive paintings scattered on the wall.

It was all rather eerie, and Joshua couldn't wait for Emmy, Amber, and Lapis to finally get here.

After seemingly hours of waiting, and just when Joshua decided he might just leave, the two women appeared, with a third cowering behind them.

"We're back!" Emmy sang out, and she moved out of the way to shove Lapis toward Joshua.

"Take a good look at her, Mr. Reynolds. This is your wife."

The woman appeared scared to death at the very sight of Joshua. Lapis turned back to Emmy and Amber, her rich black hair flowing into her eyes.

"I don't know what's happening. How did you two get to Pennsylvania. And where's Joshua?" Lapis asked fearfully.

Joshua stood dumbfounded. "You didn't tell her anything?"

Emmy looked at him defensively. "It took us long enough to track her down. I thought I'd let you do the explaining."

She shoved Lapis roughly toward Joshua, making her fall over.

Lapis cleared the hair out of her face and looked at Joshua with startled eyes. "You look so familiar." She said finally. "Do I know you from somewhere?"

"Lapis, darling, it's me." Lapis recognized the voice and instantly burst into tears.

"Joshua? What's happened? Why are you so old? Where am I?"

"You're in the future, my dear." Joshua said gently.

Lapis looked at Emmy and Amber. "You two brought me here? Why?"

"Because." Emmy said. "You must choose between him, your husband, or us, your dearest friends." Emmy smirked.

"I don't choose any of you! I want to go back home! And I still don't understand. How could this be happening?"

Lapis was verging on hysterics, and Joshua did his best to calm her down.

"It's 2021, dear. You were brought here because Emmy wants you to pledge your allegiance to her. You can either choose her, and have to stay here forever, or you can pick me, and I'll do my best to get you home."

"2021! That's almost forty years away from my time!" Lapis yelped. "Oh, Joshua, please save me! I choose you; I CHOOSE YOU!" She screamed the last bit and clung to Joshua for all she was worth.

Emmy frowned. "So, that's the way it's going to be then." She pulled a knife out of her pocket. And smiled. "I have to say, I wasn't expecting things to end this way."

Suddenly Amber wrenched the knife out of Emmy's hand.

"No, no more killing!" she shouted. She held the knife out to everyone, as if daring them to come closer.

Emmy looked visibly shaken. "Amber, we're in this together. Don't take their side."

"I have to. I won't watch my friend die." She looked at Joshua. "Your friends are alive. All but the old man. I called an ambulance for him, so his body is okay."

"Where are they?" Joshua couldn't hear himself above the pounding in his ears.

"I don't know," Amber whimpered. "Only Emmy knows."

Emmy gave an ugly smirk. "And I'll never tell." She crossed her arms over her chest. "There's nothing you can do to make me." She raised her chin in the air.

"Emmy, why are you doing this?" It was a simple question, but the way Lapis expressed it caught Emmy speechless.

"Because, because." Her body went limp. "I don't know." She deflated as she looked at Lapis.

"I just so wanted you back, and now that you're here…" her voice trailed off.

Emmy collapsed on the floor, choking in sobs. "But you didn't choose me! You didn't choose me! You chose him!"

She looked with hatred at Joshua. "This is all your fault. If I had a gun, I would shoot you in the head."

Joshua wasn't shocked, but he still felt shivers going up his spine.

He pulled his phone out of his pocket, and slowly called the Huntsville Psychiatric Hospital.

"No, you can't exile me away there! You can't, you can't, you can't…" Emmy's voice drained into little whispers.

"Amber, do you know where the watch is?"

"No, I just know she hid it downstairs somewhere."

Joshua stooped down to Emmy's level, where she lay moaning on the floor. "Do you know where the watch is? Can you tell us where it is?"

Emmy gave him a hateful stare as she lay incapacitated on the floor. "Never." She narrowed his eyes. "You've ruined my life, and I hope you never see your friends again." She continued. "You'll never find them. There's as good as dead."

The thought seemed to give her some satisfaction, and she grimaced when she heard sirens in the distance.

Slowly, she got up. "I won't go down without a fight." She muttered to herself, but her resolve weakened when she saw the stretcher coming up the stairs.

"I'm sorry it had to end this way." Amber said solemnly. She looked at Lapis.

"We'll find the watch, get you home, and then I'll help you find your friends, Joshua."

Chapter 7

Even though Lapis was eager to get home, she had a problem.

Lapis didn't want to go back to her world to die.

"Oh, I'll go back eventually. But I don't want to leave yet. Are we tempting fate if I stay here a little while?"

"I don't believe in fate. I believe in God." Joshua said.

Lapis was quick to correct herself. "Of course, that's what I meant. I don't believe in fate either. It was just an expression."

"Okay, then, you two," Amber said uncomfortably. "Lapis, you said you wanted to see the sights. Well, allow Joshua and I to give you a good time."

Joshua interjected. "Or how about Lapis helps me find my friends?" He looked at Amber pointedly. "We don't have time for games. They could be in danger."

Amber nodded. "With Emmy, I never knew. I don't know why I was her friend for so long. She had some real mental issues."

"So, you don't have any idea where they could be?"

Amber shook her head. "Absolutely no idea. However, I did notice her truck was low on gas, so she couldn't have gone far unless she refilled."

At last Lapis interjected herself. "Since I'm here, I want to be a help, too. Why don't we start by praying and asking God to help us?"

"Excellent suggestion, Lapis," Joshua said. "Go ahead." He bowed his head.

Lapis took a deep breath. "Father," she prayed. "We come to You with heavy hearts as Joshua's friends are missing. Please help us find them. Don't let them be in danger. Please, protect them, Lord. Or, if we find them to be already with You, help us to deal with the tragedy with a sense of peace, and not one of anxiety. In Your Son's name, Amen."

Amber looked up. "Wow, I already feel so much better." She said it in a surprised tone of voice.

Lapis smiled at her. "Are you a Christian, my friend?" she asked quietly.

Amber looked down. "No, but I want to be. I want what you and Joshua have. That simple measure of peace, even in adversity."

"It can be yours." Lapis then proceeded to lead Amber through a simple prayer, and Amber began to cry. "But how can He love me, a sinner such as I?"

Lapis began to soothingly sing the song "Amazing Grace," and Amber's sobs slowed. She cried out to Jesus for mercy and forgiveness, until she finally went silent.

"Am I saved now?" she asked pleadingly.

Lapis smiled gloriously. "Yes, Amber, yes you are."

Joshua bit back a grin in an attempt to remain pensive. "I welcome you to the holy family, Amber, but really, we do need to find them. Everyone get in my car, and I'll start driving around as we brainstorm."

As they walked down the steps the emergency personnel had just vacated only twenty minutes prior, Lapis spoke up.

"Tell me about them, Joshua. Tell me about your friends. I want to know everything about your life."

"Well, Angelina is my good friend. She's married, you see, and I feel no romantic inclination towards her. We're just friends. She's a good listener, and a great Christian.

"Then, there's Teresa. I don't know her as well, but what I've seen is that she's a good godly woman. She's married as well, and pretty much best friends with Angelina and Ellyn."

"Who's Ellyn?" Lapis asked, and Joshua was reminded once again of how much she had missed since she died.

"After you died, I wasn't in a relationship for years. But then I met Ellyn. We were never engaged, but very close to it."

"What happened?" Lapis asked naively, though there was no way she could have known. She sounded like a young child asking for a cookie.

"Well, Ellyn…" his voice trailed off, and he realized Amber didn't know about Ellyn either and was listening just as closely as Lapis.

"Ellyn died." He said simply. "She was murdered, by Vanessa, my cousin."

"How tragic!" Lapis exclaimed in astonishment. Amber too, let out a gasp of surprise.

Lapis softened towards him. "I'm so sorry. It must have been so hard, having two women you loved die."

"Yeah. It was. But Angelina, Teresa, and Ellyn were like three peas in a pod. They were always doing stuff together.

"Teresa and Ellyn worked together, and Angelina was later the detective on Ellyn's case. Boy, I miss them."

Lapis put a hand on her husband's shoulder. "We'll find them." She said comfortingly.

"I hope so." Joshua hadn't really been paying attention to where he was driving, and he now found himself at a dead end on a dark street.

"I guess we better turn around," Joshua started. He stared at the fading sunset. "It's going to be dark soon." He spoke. "Maybe we should just sleep on it and try again in the morning. I'm exhausted, and we're getting nowhere."

"Alright then," Amber said, "Lapis, you can stay with me at my apartment. Joshua, I have the address. Think you could plug it into your phone? I don't know how to get home from here."

When Joshua pulled out the high-tech device, Lapis' eyes widened from the back seat. "We didn't have those where I come from."

"Well, now everyone has one." Amber pulled out her own, a small phone with a yellow glittery case.

Lapis looked agape. "I guess I'll miss a lot, huh? But that's okay," she quickly added. "I'm ready to meet God."

After Joshua had typed in the address to Amber's apartment, they began on their way, and Lapis asked a question.

"Joshua, how am I going to die again? I don't think you ever told me."

Joshua gulped. "You know that pretty house your father gave us to live in."

Joshua sensed rather than saw Lapis' nod.

"Well, my dad is going to burn the house down. I already tried to stop him, but it didn't work. So, you're going to go back in for your Bible, and..." his voice trailed off.

"Never come back out, is that it?" Lapis finished for him, deflated.

"Yes, that's right. But the coroner said the cause of death was a large beam falling across your head. It's doubtful you'll feel much pain."

"But how can I go in there knowing what I do?"

"I don't know." Joshua answered honestly. "I just know I don't want to be there when it happens again, for a third time."

At this point, Joshua was only a few minutes away from his destination, and all dialogue ceased when Amber's apartment came into view.

It wasn't how Joshua pictured it. Somehow, he had imagined it looking more like his own, the dingy, faded building with the graffiti that he called home.

But this place was more like a hotel. And Joshua could instantly see that Lapis was going to be a lot more comfortable here than she would be at his place.

As all three walked into the lobby, both Amber and Lapis stopped in front of him. "It might seem kind of weird for you to come upstairs with us." Amber said, embarrassed. "So, we should probably just say good night here."

"I hadn't even thought of that," Joshua admitted, scratching the back of his head. "Guess I better get back." He said nervously, and he slowly walked away, backwards.

"See you tomorrow, dear!" Lapis called, and she received some strange looks from some nearby onlookers.

At least she hadn't said, "husband." That would have really attracted attention.

As Joshua walked out to his car, he smiled to himself, despite all that he had just gone through, and all he would still have to overcome.

He was here, with his wife, who was probably forty years younger than he was at this time, trying to track down his friends, who he only knew were alive because his former enemy had told him.

What a conundrum.

He only wondered now how it would all be solved.

As Joshua drove, he wondered just how Emmy had managed to kidnap his friends.

First of all, how had Emmy known where everyone lived? Sure, the internet probably played a huge role in things, but certainly there was more than one Angelina Carmen in their district of Pennsylvania.

Second, how had she managed to convince the women to leave their homes? Surely Emmy couldn't have transported a gun to Angelina's office, where Angelina most certainly was. And Teresa? He knew that Heidi and Isabelle-.

Wait. Isabelle.

The baby. Where on earth was she? Amber didn't mention anything about a baby, and while it was possible Teresa had managed to snag her up, it was even more likely Isabelle had been down for a nap at the time and was thus still at the Morgan home.

It was getting dark, but Joshua couldn't just leave Isabelle alone. Granted, Mr. Morgan was probably there, but Joshua didn't want to take any chances.

Joshua knew in the dark it would be harder to find Teresa's home, especially because he hadn't gone there very many times since the Morgan family had moved.

But he had to make sure Isabelle was okay.

He drove restlessly, making turns involuntarily as if he were a robot. Finally, he stopped in front of the Morgan house. It was just as he remembered it. Vaguely.

But I just visited here a few days ago. How are things not more familiar? Joshua wondered to himself.

Maybe this was the wrong house. But no, the well-remembered 107 on the mailbox told him this was the place.

Things look different in the dark.

As he walked up the driveway, Joshua noticed that no lights were on the inside of the house.

However, he could plainly see Mr. Morgan's car in the driveway.

Mr. Morgan. What was his first name? Richard? Ted? Pretty sure it was Ted.

He rang the doorbell, and heard a slurred, "Coming!" as if someone had just woken up.

The door slowly opened, and Joshua turned to see Ted standing there.

Ted looked awful. Like he hadn't slept in days. "Ted!" Joshua exclaimed. "Are you okay? You look terrible."

Ted looked at him in wonderment. "First of all, do you know Teresa's missing? I haven't been able to contact her. I called the police, but they won't do anything until twenty-four hours have gone by. Second, I'm not Ted. I'm Adam."

Joshua mentally kicked himself in the forehead. Adam? How had he forgotten? He was getting too old for this.

But he needed to put Adam's fears somewhat to rest. "I don't know where Teresa or Heidi is—"

"Wait, Heidi's gone too? I thought she was at Angelina's."

"Angelina's also gone."

Adam tugged at his hair. "What is the world coming to? And how are we going to find them?"

"That's where the good news comes in. We don't know where they are, but we know someone who does."

"Who?"

"A woman. Her name is Emmy. I'm not sure what her last name is. She was admitted to the psychiatric hospital this evening for threatening to kill me."

"What else have I missed?"

Joshua then went on to tell him everything that had gone on, starting with the watch, and finishing with the kidnappings of Angelina, Teresa, and Heidi.

"So how do we get them back?"

"Well, based on what Amber said, she didn't drop them off far away. We looked at the gas gauge in her car and it was near empty."

"So, they're close by to that house you were staying at. Okay, wow, so what do we do next?"

Joshua said, "I came here because I wanted to make sure Isabelle was safe, and that she hadn't been taken. Is she all right?"

"Yeah, yeah. She was screaming at the top of her lungs when I came home, but I've always been a favorite of hers. I got her settled down pretty quickly."

Joshua was nodding his head. "Good. Now, I have a lot of planning to do, so I'm going back to my apartment to get some sleep. Though you look like you need more sleep than I do."

"Don't I know it. Hey, you have my phone number, right? Call me in the morning and let me know your plans."

"Will do. All right, see you soon."

As Joshua pulled out of the driveway and drove away, he was glad to add another member to his team.

He wasn't sure what Adam did for a living, but hopefully he'd be able to take a few days off from work to get this whole situation taken care of. Especially if the police weren't going to do anything.

Joshua slept well that night. He had exhausted plan after plan, and he was very tired. When he woke up the next morning, he thought about his landlord's kindness, how he allowed him to stay a few more weeks. Joshua hadn't even had to explain the situation to him. Overall, his landlord wasn't that bad of a guy.

Joshua plugged Amber's residence address into his phone and drove there quickly. He wanted to get there as quickly as possible.

As luck would have it, or maybe it was divine intervention, Lapis and Amber were already waiting outside for him.

He had texted Amber earlier that he would pick them up, right before he went to pick up Adam, so that way they could all conference together and decide what to do.

Lapis and Amber both got in the back seat of the car. "Good morning, ladies." Joshua said grimly.

"Good morning," they responded in unison.

"So, what's the plan?" Lapis asked.

Joshua was frustrated. "Why does everyone keep asking me if I have a plan? I don't know any better than you."

Lapis was taken aback, and Joshua apologized. "Sorry," he murmured gruffly.

Lapis lifted her chin, and Joshua saw that stubborn glint in her eyes from the rearview mirror.

"It's quite alright. It's been a rough time for all of us. Now we need to focus on solutions. I'm confident we'll find your friends."

"At least you are. I have my doubts." Joshua grumbled.

Lapis looked earnestly at the back of his head. "I prayed, and asked God to help us find your friends. I feel confident He'll answer my prayer, and the prayer of all of us."

"I prayed too and felt peace as well." Amber piped up.

"Good! I'm so glad." Lapis grasped Amber's hands in her own.

Amber spoke again. "I think we should split up. I have a car, and I suppose your friend probably has a car, right Joshua? Then you and Lapis can just stay together."

"Sounds good to me. How far away does your friend live from here, Joshua?"

"About five minutes. He said he would be ready to leave at 8:00 am, and it's 7:55 now. So, there should be plenty of time. Did Emmy give you any hints about where Joshua's friends might be, Amber? Anything, any at all?"

Amber shook her head. "Absolutely nothing that I can think of. I'm sorry I'm not more help."

"Trust me, with the police on our side, things will be a lot easier. I don't understand why they aren't involved now. A child is missing." Joshua let his voice rise a little.

"It's okay," Lapis soothed, and she found herself staring out the window. "Oh, think of that blue sky. And the wonderful trees. God made all that. He numbered all the hairs on our heads. He knows everything about us, and He knows exactly where Angelina and Teresa and Heidi are. Isn't that wonderful?"

Joshua went from trusting God to doubting Him. Now was one of those doubting moments. "Sure wish He would just tell us. I can imagine them being in plain sight somewhere."

Joshua pulled into Adam's driveway and was happy to see him already waiting outside. Adam immediately jumped up and ran to the car window.

"Josh? Mind if I call you that? Can I get in the passenger side, or what?"

"Sure, just get in."

Adam's lanky body had a hard time fitting into the front seat. He pushed the car seat back.

Then he turned back to the two girls in the backseat.

"How are you? You're Amber, right?" Amber lifted a milky brown hand to shake his own.

"And you're the Lapis I've heard so much about. Lapis Lazuli, right?"

Lapis looked embarrassed. "Well, in my old world, it was Lapis Reynolds, but yes, that is my maiden name."

"Fascinating. Well, forget the pleasantries. What are we all thinking as far as a plan goes?"

"Well, I thought we would get breakfast at a restaurant somewhere, and we'd discuss it."

Amber spoke up. "I don't want to eat somewhere. I'm not hungry, and I can guarantee you no one else is either." She looked pointedly at all of them.

"So, like I was saying earlier, I say we split up. Which means, Joshua's friend, I don't think I caught your name, that you need to hop out of this car, get in your own, and start looking. And you, Joshua, need to drive me right back to my apartment so I can get my car. I've said my piece. Now let's discuss." Amber seemed out of breath after the long sentiment.

Adam was looking quizzically at her. "Well, my name's Adam, in case you're wondering. And I think your idea is a good one. What do you say, Josh? Should we cast a vote?"

Joshua shook his head. "No, nothing like that. I think we should go with Amber's idea, since it seems like the only option. And I want us to establish that I'm not the leader here. We're all on equal playing ground."

Lapis spoke for the first time. "No, I think you kind of *are* the leader. You tell us what to do, and we do it. I, for one, am a follower, and I know Amber is too. I'm not sure about you, Adam, but Joshua is the naturally selected leader, and I think we should stick with it."

Joshua sighed. "Fine. Not that it matters anyway." He waited for Adam to unbuckle his seatbelt and grab his own car keys from out of his pocket.

"Don't go anywhere without them," he said as an offer of explanation.

Joshua waited some more until Adam got in his car and gave the thumbs up signal through his window. "Which way should I go?"

Lapis opened her window. "Wherever God tells you!" she shouted.

"Will do!" Adam called back.

Joshua headed out, back to Amber's apartment.

Something clicked in Joshua's head. Suddenly, in the middle of a cross section, he squealed on the brakes and turned onto a side road.

"This isn't the way to my apartment," Amber frowned.

"I know where they are," Joshua answered in reply.

Chapter 8

"Where? How?" Lapis asked.

"It's just a guess," Joshua said through gritted teeth. "But I have a feeling they're at my apartment. Like I said, just a guess, but something's off with my landlord. He didn't even ask me why I needed the extra weeks, and he's always so particular about that. Almost as if he already knew. Something's up with that."

"So. We need to call Adam. Tell him what your hypothesis is." Amber stated.

"Don't get scientific on me." Joshua grumbled. "But I think you're right. We need to let Adam know immediately." He handed Amber his phone. "Think you can take it from there?"

"Yeah, of course." Amber busily set to work finding Adam's contact on Joshua's phone.

Joshua continued to drive, more resolute than ever that his "hypothesis" was correct.

Amber had Adam on the phone, and Lapis watched with wide eyes as the two spoke to each other.

"Joshua thinks they may be at his apartment due to some funny antics from his landlord, Mr., what did you say his name was again, Joshua?"

"Charlie. I don't think I ever caught a last name."

Amber rolled her eyes, still with Adam on the phone. "Men. How long have you been living there, and you don't know your landlord's name?" She returned to Adam. "So, head back to Joshua's apartment. You said it was called Lakeview? You know where that is, right? Cause I sure don't."

Adam appeared thoughtful. "That's east of my house, right?"

Joshua spoke into the phone. "Yeah, I think so."

"I had the same intuition to head east. You said your apartment building complex, Lakeview, is owned by a Charlie?"

"Yeah," Joshua replied. "You know more about him?"

"Maybe. I had this friend some years back. He told me that he always wanted to be a landlord. Don't know why. The power, probably. Anyway, he said he would name his pick of apartments Lakeview, because there's such a nice view of the lake nearby. His name was Charlie, also."

"Ever catch a last name?" Amber asked.

"Sure, it's Lazuli. Hey, maybe he's related to you, Lapis."

Lapis was tugging at her thick black strands of hair. "Oh, no, oh no, oh no," she kept murmuring to herself.

Amber put a hand on Lapis' knee, the phone still in hand. "What is it? What is it, Lapis?"

"Uncle Charlie," she whispered. "Convicted of murder. He escaped from prison, and no one knew where he went. I would have never thought of him coming here, to Huntsville, to be close to my dad. They were brothers, you know."

Amber soothingly rubbed her back. "You get all that, Adam?"

Adam's tone was grim. "Somehow I think we're in a lot more trouble than I initially thought."

Amber said, "Is there anyway Mr. Fritz is connected in all this?"

"Mr. Fritz? Who's that? The banker guy?"

Joshua nodded, even though he knew Adam couldn't see it. "Aka Mr. Lazuli, Lapis' dad."

"Whoa, whoa, whoa. Let me get this straight. But wasn't Emmy and Amber working for Mr. Fritz, like you told me last night?"

"That's right. But Mr. Lazuli, Frank, couldn't be part of all this. Ellyn helped him to get saved."

"Ellyn? How does Ellyn fit into all this? Sorry, I'm asking a lot of questions, but I just need to understand."

"No time," Joshua said, suddenly tired. "The point is Frank could have been lying about being saved just so Ellyn wouldn't worry about him anymore."

"Why would she worry about him in the first place?" Adam asked over the phone.

"Because, he had a miniature stroke in her house."

"I'm not even going to ask what you were doing at Ellyn's house."

"Thanks. So, now, we may have to stop two criminals from wreaking major havoc on our friends."

"My dad isn't a criminal. And he wouldn't do something like what you're accusing him of doing. I know my dad better than all of you, and he just wouldn't do something like that."

"You may not know your dad as well as you think. He pulled a gun on me, Lapis. And shot me in the shoulder. Threatened to shoot me if I didn't give him the watch."

The watch.

That stupid hunk of metal that had nearly ruined his life.

More than once.

He wished he never accepted it from Peter. And now Peter was dead.

What a life he had.

Back to the conversation at hand.

Lapis' audible gasp shocked him. But then again, he guessed it shouldn't have. Everyone thought their dad was perfect until they grew up and realized how much of a cad he sometimes was.

Like his dad.

But back to the present.

"So, what if these two Lazuli's are in cahoots with one another? What then?"

"Then we have to stop them." Joshua pulled up into the apartment's parking lot. "Now."

"As far as I can recollect, I'm five minutes out. Wait for me, okay? And don't you think you'd better call the police?" Adam asked.

Joshua looked sternly ahead. "No," was all he said.

When Adam arrived precisely seven minutes later, (Joshua counted) the trio was gathered outside Joshua's car, trying to appear unsuspicious. And failing miserably.

Amber was picking at her faded yellow nails, Lapis was pulling her hair and shaking uncontrollably. And Joshua was looking down at his silent phone, pretending to stare at something when in reality he was staring at nothing.

They all glanced up when Adam pulled into the empty spot beside Joshua's vehicle.

"I'm here." He pointed out the obvious.

"Wow, that's self-explanatory." Joshua said sarcastically. "Come on, let's go."

Adam stopped him.

"We need to have a plan before we just go in and confront them. And who's to say that they're even there? Come on, man. Think through this."

"I have thought through this and I'm going in now. Whether you're coming with me, or not."

He made his way to the door, and the three trailed behind him.

As he walked inside, he was struck with the sinisterness of this place. How had he never noticed it before? There was an evil aura, lurking around every corner and in every shadow.

Joshua went directly to Charlie Lazuli's office. He pushed open the door and wasn't surprised to see Frank Lazuli standing over him with a gun in his hand. Charlie practically shook with fear.

"Daddy, what are you doing?" Lapis asked tentatively, and Frank towards them with a look of disbelief. "Lapis, is that you, sweetheart?"

"Yes, Daddy, it's me." She walked over to him, putting her arm around him. "What are you doing?" she asked again.

"Uh, I'm, uh." Frank seemed at a loss for words.

In a lightning quick motion, Lapis had retrieved the gun out of her father's hands before he could protest. She pointed it at him, and then at Charlie.

"I want someone to tell me what's going on. Where are my husband's friends?"

Charlie looked with a smirk at Lapis. "I'll never tell." The near exact words that Emmy had spoken.

Could it be some kind of joke?

Charlie then proceeded to produce a gun of his own. Lapis quickly handed her gun to Joshua. At least he knew how to use one.

Joshua tossed the gun into the air with his left hand, catching it with his left. "Where are they?" he said quietly. Then, more loudly, "Where are they!?"

Charlie appeared unfazed.

Frank still looked dumbfounded. He stared at his daughter with a queer look on his face. "How can you be here? That must mean you," he turned to Joshua, "still have the watch."

He looked at Amber. "And what are you doing with them, honey? You belong with us."

"No, I've been saved by the blood of Jesus Christ. Unlike you. Liar."

"I did what I had to do." Frank rolled his eyes and shrugged.

Lapis stared in horror at her father. "Daddy, what are you saying? You don't believe in Jesus?"

"Never bought into it, I guess. Why? Because you did?"

"I didn't buy into anything, Dad." Joshua detected a cold edge in Lapis' tone of voice.

"I believe with all my heart that Jesus died for me. How can you not?"

"Never got the gene, I guess. But that's not important. What's important is that you get your little husband to hand over the gun."

At Frank's condescending manner, Lapis snapped. "You're not the dad I knew and loved. You're nothing but a sinister copycat. I hate you. I really do!"

Frank looked crestfallen. Like the love of his daughter was all he had left to live for.

Charlie had continued to smirk the entire time. "Enough, enough." He said finally. "Let's get down to business, shall we?"

In a lightning fast motion, he withdrew a gun and then proceeded to shoot Amber in the heart.

"No!" Lapis screamed, and Joshua logged a bullet in Charlie's head. He slumped over.

"She isn't breathing." Lapis looked stunned. And frightened. Like a little girl who just lost her favorite doll.

Lapis lay limp by her side. Adam sidled up to her, putting his arm around her shoulders.

"You shouldn't have done that." Joshua didn't know if Adam was talking to him or the corpse of Charlie.

Frank ran over to Charlie, then glared at Joshua. "You kill my daughter, and then you kill my brother. Now I'll kill you."

Frank grabbed the gun out of his still brother's hand and raised it at Joshua. He felt a warm, pounding sensation in his chest, and suddenly everything went black.

Joshua awoke to the sound of beeping noises. All around him. He dared to open his eyes.

Great. He was in a hospital. Again. At least he wouldn't have Emmy for a nurse. He grinned despite himself.

"Oh good," someone said. "You're awake."

Joshua turned over and found that the motion was drastically painful.

"Don't try to move." The voice said. "You're safe here."

It was Lapis' voice. She really shouldn't be here.

"The watch." Joshua moaned, and the words came out in throaty gasps.

"Don't talk." Lapis walked over to him and touched his graying hair. "You need to save your strength."

"But...you need to get out of here." His voice grew stronger. "Take the watch and go."

Lapis looked at him stubbornly. She smiled. "What happens if I say no?"

Joshua tried to smile, but he grimaced instead. "What's happened?" he strained himself to ask.

Lapis' gaze clouded. "Oh, nothing much. Turns out Adam called the police while he was in his car on the way to Lakeview. They came in on Adam's signal."

"Which was?"

Lapis laughed. "Shouting for them to come in there."

"So...then what happened?"

"Well, my father was taken into custody, and he's being questioned as we speak. You know his shot was inches away from your heart. You could be dead, you know."

"Yeah. I know. I guess God's not done with me yet."

Lapis looked out the window. "No, I guess He's not."

"What's on your mind?"

"Oh, just that my whole childhood was a lie created by my father. Sometimes I'm not sure I even want to get back to it."

"But you have to." Joshua said. "I'm sure there's dozens of search parties looking for you right now."

"Comforting thought, I guess. That I'm cared about. I guess I really should go..." Her words trailed off, and Joshua thought about what it would mean losing her again.

"We still haven't found my friends. Please stay."

Lapis looked at him strangely. "I don't begrudge you for this, but I think I've lost your heart."

"What? What does that mean?"

"Your heart was broken a second time when you lost Ellyn. And now, the other half of your heart is buried with her, not me."

"That's not true. I love you." Joshua defended himself passionately.

"Oh, there's no question of that. I love you as well, my darling. It's just that, well, you don't love me the same way anymore.

"And that's totally fine. I can just go back to my younger Joshua and receive that love once again."

Suddenly she picked up the watch and fingered it in her hands. "What's the deal, Joshua Reynolds?" she said softly.

"What?" Joshua struggled to hear.

"What's the deal. You remember, that's how I always used to greet you when we were kids. 'What's the deal, Joshua Reynolds?' Do you remember your reply?"

"How could I forget? It was so stupid. 'And how do you do, Lapis Lazuli?'"

Lapis laughed. "You remember how you always used to bow after that? I always found that hilarious." She wore a sad smile.

Lapis looked down at the watch, then walked over to Joshua's bedside. "I love you," she whispered to him gently.

"What are you going to do with the watch once you get back to your home?"

"I don't know. Probably bury it so my father will never find it. Got any suggestions?"

"No, that idea sounds pretty good."

Lapis looked at him tenderly. She stroked the watch gently. "Good bye, old boy."

"Goodbye, old girl."

And then she was gone, without so much as a trace.

The watch was gone too. He was finally free of that pesky thing.

What was it Lapis had said about Ellyn? Had his heart really been hers this whole time?

If only he could be sure.

But there was no way he would ever see Ellyn again. At least not on this earth.

And with that astonishing realization, Joshua collapsed in horrendous sobs that shook his very being.

A few hours later, Adam walked into the room. Only to discover that Lapis was no longer there.

"Where's Lapis?"

"Gone." Joshua half-whimpered.

"What do you mean, gone? Is she down in the cafeteria or something?"

"No. She went back to her world."

"What? Did she take the watch with her?" At Joshua's nod, Adam stiffened. "Mr. Lazuli's isn't going to be happy about this new development, you know. We used Lapis as a bargaining chip to get him to talk. Why'd she leave?"

"She just felt it was time to go. I didn't have the heart to stop her."

"You know Amber's dead, right?"

"Yeah, why?"

"You think that's why Lapis left, maybe? Couldn't take the pain?"

"Maybe." Joshua said listlessly.

"What's wrong with you? We have Lazuli, an attempted murderer. He's almost ready to reveal where Teresa and Angelina are! Why aren't you more enthusiastic?"

"I just lost my wife, okay? Again!" Joshua shouted as loud as his raspy voice would allow.

"I've lost everyone," he murmured.

"No, you haven't. You haven't lost me, or Angelina, or even Teresa. We'll get them back; I know we will."

"But at what cost?" Joshua half-shouted. He allowed himself to block out Adam's hissing words and wandered off to a tumultuous sleep, which wasn't really sleep at all, more like a nightmare.

And he would never wake up.

Chapter 9

Joshua had a better outlook on things when next he awoke.

Adam had gone home that night, but he returned in the morning, also positive about the day's events.

"I'm convinced we'll find them soon. We have the police to back us up now, you know."

Joshua grunted. "That's good, I guess. Too bad I'll be out of commission for a while."

Adam smiled. "That doesn't necessarily mean you can't help. We're thinking they're located on the apartment building property, and you probably know it a lot better than we all do. I know you're stuck here, but you can give us tips. That is, if you're willing to help."

Joshua appeared taken aback for a second. Of course he wanted to help! But he immediately recovered his cool gaze. "I'll do whatever I can," he said earnestly. "I'll not rest until they're found."

"Then let's get this day started with a cup of coffee." Adam exited the room.

Joshau wracked his brain, thinking of all the places the two women and the small girl may be.

They had to be in one of the apartments. That much was certain. But which one? Joshua hoped the police enlisted search-and-rescue dogs to find his friends quicker.

Joshua remembered the promise he had made to Ellyn; his vow to watch over Rain and her offspring if something were to happen to her.

Joshua may not have been able to save Rain, but he would do his best to save Heidi. If she wasn't already gone.

But Joshua couldn't let himself think that way. They would recover them. And Joshua would see Heidi again. He could keep his promise, he knew he could.

Joshua thought about how hard this must be on Adam. To have his wife missing-and to not know where she was, or even if she was alive...

And what of Angelina's husband? He hadn't heard anything from him. As far as Joshua knew, Angelina didn't have any children, but he'd been wrong before. These inconsistencies made Joshua want to question Angelina about her home life.

Next, he wondered about Emmy and Charlie Lazuli in cahoots with each other. He thought about how that was all connected, then decided he didn't want to go down that rabbit hole.

No, right now, he needed to concentrate on getting the girls back.

And building his own strength.

A few moments later, Adam came back in, two cups of coffee balancing in his hands. He placed one cup on the night table beside Joshua bed; the other he kept in his hand. "Searchers have already started searching the apartment complex. I just wanted to stop here and see if you had any leads to give us."

Joshua shook his head mournfully. "Sorry, Adam. I can't think of anything. The best I can think us is to continue questioning Frank Lazuli, and maybe he'll accidently give something away."

"I doubt that, but we have to try, don't we?" Adam gave a sad smile, and his eyes stared longingly out the window. "What I wouldn't give to have Teresa in my arms right now." He sighed. "But maybe that will never happen."

"Don't talk like that! We'll get them back," said Joshua gruffly, hiding his inward pain. He couldn't stand failing and losing Heidi to some unknown force.

"Are they going to use the dogs?" Joshua asked his friend.

"Not sure." Adam rubbed his chin. "Hey, I hadn't thought of that. I better run home and find something of Teresa's. And I'm sure I have Heidi's hairbrush or something somewhere. It's got her scent all over it."

Excited now, Adam rushed out the door, "Sorry to cut things off, buddy, but thanks for the idea!"

Adam raced out, leaving Joshua in his wake. Joshua looked at the door longingly. If only there were some ways for him to help.

He sighed. But no. He was stuck here, just as he would be for a good, long, while.

Adam felt bad he had left his friend all alone. But certainly, the police would need some kind of clothing or something to help identify where exactly his wife and friends were.

Oh, what he wouldn't give to be holding his darling right now.

Adam walked out to the car, grabbed his keys from his pocket in the process.

Then he carefully drove as fast as he could out to the Morgan home. Racing along, he grabbed a few of Heidi's things, and stuck them in a plastic bag.

Then he grabbed another bag and tenderly transported Teresa's clothing to the carrier.

This done, he went back out to his car, placed the things carefully on the passenger seat, and drove out of the driveway into the oncoming traffic.

Joshua watched cars going by from his hospital window and imagined one of them was Adam's.

He knew Adam would probably be at the police station by now and knowing that only gave him a greater desire to get in on the action.

Maybe he could convince someone he needed to go outside. But no, that was impossible. However, it didn't hurt to try.

He pressed the nurse-calling button.

Almost immediately a nurse came in, wearing green scrubs, and caring latex gloves in her right hand.

Joshua shivered. He hated latex gloves.

But that was beside the point. Before he could get a word out, the nurse, whose name tag read Lily, spoke to him first.

"You ready for some more pain meds?" she asked sweetly, and Joshua was once again reminded that some seemingly sweet people were twisted and cruel on the inside.

"No, nothing like that." Joshua started. He had almost forgotten the killer pain in his chest where he had been shot.

"Actually, I was wondering if I could have a brief leave of absence from the hospital here. You see—"

"Your friends are missing, and you want to help find them. Is that it?"

Joshua nodded.

"So, what can I do for you?"

"Let me leave so I can help."

"And how do you propose I do that? Not only would I be putting my job on the line, you're in no condition to be traveling, wheelchair or not."

Joshua felt defeated. "So, there's nothing you can do?"

She shook her head. "I'm afraid not. I'm sympathetic, really, I am, but there's just nothing I can do."

As she walked away, Joshua gave a small sigh of disappointment. So, he really was stuck here.

He pulled out his phone and dialed Adam's number.

Adam gave the police officer on duty his "evidence" and then hurried to the apartments where he could begin searching.

His phone rang. He looked at the caller ID and found it was Joshua. Hurriedly, he accepted the call.

"Hey, Josh. I just got here. What's up?"

"Well, I tried to get out of here, but that didn't work."

"What, did you bribe one of the nurses?" Adam joked.

"Why are you in such a good mood?" Joshua complained.

"I don't know. I just have a good feeling about today. Like we're going to find them."

"Boy, I sure hope so. Have you been praying? I know I have."

"Nonstop. Look, I've got to go. I need to speak to the lead here. See what I can do to help."

"No problem. Thanks for the update."

Adam clicked off the phone and made his way up to the head of the search team.

"So, what can I do to help?" he asked cheerfully.

The lead smiled. "I like your attitude sir. I take it you're Adam Morgan, right? I'm Rose Aureate. Good to meet you."

They shook hands, and Adam immediately got down to business. "What can I do to help?"

"Well, police should be arriving here soon with their search and rescue dogs. They're coming with a search warrant, so right now we're just scanning the premises, waiting for them to get here."

Rose checked her watch. "They shouldn't be long in coming."

Adam smiled in relief. "Good. I guess I'll just dally around a little bit, get to know the area better."

"Sounds good. Let me know if you need anything."

"Of course." Adam walked away slowly, wishing he could be with his wife now. Where was she? And where was Heidi, or Angelina?

He hoped he would find out soon.

After what seemed an eternity, police personnel pulled into the parking lot, and stepped out of their vehicles, search dogs in tow.

A police officer nearby was holding some of Teresa's things, and the dog immediately took off in one direction. Several others followed.

Adam watched in amazement as the dogs pawed at the lobby door, aching to get inside.

A police officer came in and knocked down the door, allowing the dogs inside. Adam followed behind at a respectful distance.

He saw inside as the dogs headed to the office Adam, Amber, and Joshua had vacated just a few days earlier.

They couldn't be in there. How would they have not seen them? Still, the dogs pushed on, before stopping at a desk drawer and clambering to paw it open.

The officer did it for them, and Adam could see some clothes of some sort peeking out of the drawer.

He immediately recognized Teresa's black sweatshirt; the comfy one she wore on a regular basis.

His heart caught in his throat.

The police officer seemed to notice him for the first time. "This is a restricted area. You're not allowed in here."

Adam carefully maneuvered his way back outside, but that didn't keep him from going around the office building, and carefully looking into a window while the police did their work.

He couldn't make out what the officer was saying, but he saw him put Teresa's sweatshirt right up to the dogs' nose.

The dogs immediately started into a trot down the hallway, and they were soon hidden from view.

Adam walked back out to the front of the building, where he watched the dogs emerge and quickly run over to the back of the building where he had just been.

However, they continued. Straight into the woods.

To a shed neither Adam, nor anyone on the search team, had yet noticed.

This had to be where they were. Had to be.

Adam followed along at a brisk pace, despite what the officer had said about staying away.

If his Teresa was in there, he needed to be the one to find her.

As people from Rose's search team crowded around the outbuilding, the police officers had to holler to be heard. "Back away from the premises!" One shouted. Soon, they had the officers separated from the civilians, and all was quiet.

That's when Adam heard it. A scuffling noise inside the shed, and a slow, steady, ticking noise.

"There's a bomb in there!" An officer shouted. "Get the bomb crew out here stat!"

Adam gasped inwardly. So his wife *was* in danger. The crew couldn't get out there fast enough.

He overheard the officers talking.

"I think if we open this door, the bomb is going to blow."

"It's going to blow one way or another, it's just a matter of time. That bomb is counting down."

"How long do you think we have?" That was Rose.

"Not long. They've been shut up in there for a few days. Could be another few days, could be a matter of minutes. Don't know."

Adam finally spoke up. "Why aren't they speaking?" He sounded dumb even to his own ears.

The officer shook his head. "Chances are they're tied up and their mouths are taped shut. That's my guess."

Fair enough. It was better than the alternative for why they weren't talking. They may be dead.

But that shuffling noise still going on in the shed allowed for something living being in there.

Adam only hoped it wasn't a bat or something. That would be a letdown.

But something told Adam they were in there. He decided to call Joshua.

As soon as Joshua picked up, Adam dived right into his story. "I think they may be in a shed a little ways off the property. The police have a bomb crew coming to disengage a bomb they think might be there."

"A bomb!" Joshua yelled into the phone. Adam winced at the noise.

"Yes, a bomb, maybe. Once the crew gets here, we'll know for sure."

From Joshua's end, things were going good and bad. He had convinced a nurse to let him go outside to get some sun. At least that was the excuse he gave.

The bad news was that was far as he had got. No offers to drive him someplace. Just letting him sit in the sun, while a nurse waited for him nearby.

That was where he was when he got the phone call.

"How will the crew know there's a bomb?" Joshua asked. Stupid question. They had their methods.

Adam didn't even answer the question. "They're here." He said simply. "I'll let you go, but I'll try to keep you up—"

There was a thundering crash that came from the other end of the phone, and Adam's end disconnected.

Joshua stared in confusion at the phone. He tried calling back, but Adam didn't pick up.

It was only then he realized the bomb must have been engaged.

He only hoped all his friends weren't dead.

ADAM WAS KNOCKED OFF his feet by the blast. The shed burst into flames, and Adam watched his wife go up with it.

But wait. There. He saw someone crawling out. Barely.

But others noticed it too.

"There's someone there!" someone shouted.

Adam found his feet moving automatically forward.

The next thing he knew, he was racing toward the shed, ignoring the ringing of the phone in his pocket, and then Teresa was in his arms, sobbing as he wrenched the tape off her burned face.

They held each other together closely.

Chapter 10

Adam didn't see the trained firemen leading the burned Angelina and Heidi away from the wreckage.

He heard them.

Their muttered wailings, Heidi's furtive cry for her mother. It broke his heart to pieces.

But that didn't matter right now. What mattered was the woman in his arms.

"I knew you would find us." Teresa whispered through cracked lips.

"What happened?" Adam had to ask.

"We were kidnapped, all three of us," Teresa rasped. "She held us at gunpoint. The nurse did. She wasn't very smart. She still had her nametag on."

"What was her name?"

"Emmy, the name tag read."

"Don't worry, she's in an intensive care unit at Huntsville Psychiatric."

"Where I work?"

"Yes." That was all Adam could manage to reply. He held Teresa closely, daring anyone close by to disentangle them.

Everyone stayed far away from the private moment.

"You need an ambulance." Adam looked at his wife's burns and...bite marks?

"What did they do to you?"

Teresa gave a small laugh. "She was a crazy one, that nurse was. She bit us, scratched us, anything that would get us to denounce our God. She went on and on about her best friend, how God had abandoned her, so on and so forth. You ever heard of someone named Lapis?"

"I guess you've missed a lot. I'll fill you in later. For now, it's so good to have you back." He kissed her on the forehead, where she wasn't burned, and thanked God for saving her.

"Adam!"

The voice was distinguishable among the many people. Joshua.

He was breathless, and on his feet, but he was there.

The two grasped each other's arms, leaving Teresa momentarily on the ground alone. But she was smiling big.

"How did you get here?" Adam asked quickly, looking around to see if Joshua was being chased by hospital personnel.

Joshua laughed. "That nurse changed her mind. She called me a cab and helped me escape. I can't imagine why she did it, unless she had friends of her own. Really good friends, like you guys."

He seemed to notice Teresa for the first time. "Teresa! You're safe! Are the others okay too?" Teresa smiled, getting up gingerly from the ground.

"Everyone's fine. But if you want to make sure, go over to that ambulance over there."

She began walking in that direction, but Adam stopped her.

"Save your strength," he said, and he proceeded to lift her up into his arms.

She giggled like a little girl, obviously enjoying the attention even as she winced in pain.

Joshua felt the sting of his chest wound as he marched along beside Adam. Weren't they a pair?

But he didn't care. If Heidi and Angelina were safe, nothing else mattered.

Joshua was transported back to the hospital, along with Heidi, Angelina, and Teresa. Several ambulances came and picked them up, but they remained in contact via their phones, which Emmy for some reason hadn't taken from them.

"Why didn't you try to call emergency services?" Joshua asked Angelina. The phone didn't express any answer for a moment, then Angelina texted back.

"Couldn't. My phone was in my back pocket, and I couldn't reach it. Neither could Teresa."

Joshua supposed that made sense.

When they checked in at the hospital, he was being treated for his chest wound, and the others being cared for their burns, Joshua finally had time to call Angelina. He had an important question he wanted and needed to ask.

"Angelina," he started, not sure what to say. He could hear the beeping of monitors in the background.

"Are you in a lot of pain?" Might as well get the pleasantries out of the way.

"Yeah." Angelina sounded sleepy, and for a moment, Joshua wondered if he was making a mistake in calling her.

"I do have a quick question I'd like to ask, if that's okay."

"Shoot."

"Where's your husband? Why isn't he here looking after you?"

Dead silence on Angelina's end. Then, "Why do you ask?" Obviously, Joshua had triggered a nerve.

"It just seems like you would want to have him close to you, especially in this difficult time, you know?"

"I wish he were here." Angelina said. Joshua could hear tears in her voice. "But he wouldn't come. He's never coming back. He left me a few months ago."

Joshua tried to keep his shock in check. "Why didn't you tell anybody?" He finally managed to whisper.

"I'm in my seventies, Joshua. I really should have retired long ago. How would you feel in you spent more than half of your life with a man that suddenly up and left? You wouldn't want that broadcast to the whole world, would you?"

Joshua sighed. "I guess not. Still, I wish you would have been able to tell me."

Now it was Angelina's turn to sigh. "I like you a lot, Joshua, really, I do. But I was so embarrassed..." her words trailed off, and at her rhythmic breathing Joshua realized she had fallen asleep.

He hung up the phone. And wondered, now, with Angelina's husband gone, where that put them in their relationship.

Joshua had always been careful, but he also really liked Angelina. Maybe, with Angelina's permission, they could take it one step further.

That is, if she was ready to move on. He knew healing could take time.

It was a few months later, with everyone out of the hospital, that Joshua received another surprise of his life.

In the months leading up to this surprise, Lakeview had come under new management, and the new landlord had found no reason why Joshua couldn't stay.

As it turned out, Charlie Lazuli had only ordered Joshua out on the account that he thought Joshua knew too much.

Which may have been a little true.

But with his home back, Joshua felt like a new person.

Angelina had agreed that she would like to take things a step further, but now Joshua was the one with reservations.

Was it okay that he was finally happy even though two of his most beloved darlings were dead?

So the surprise came.

Joshua had just finished making dinner, and now was cleaning up his single dirty dish.

"Hello, Joshua," a voice said from behind him.

He looked backwards, scared out of his wits. Until he saw who it was.

His beloved Lapis, with her beautiful dark hair, watch in hand.

"But I thought you would be dead by now. Pardon the bluntness."

Lapis laughed. "Turns out, Emmy got the timing all wrong. I still have a few months yet to live."

"So, are you coming to stay?"

"Me? No, I just wanted to see you one more time. Before I bury the watch forever. And I brought someone with me I think you might want to see."

She looked towards the doorway, and Ellyn stepped out.

She smiled beautifully, and suddenly both women were in Joshua's arms, all three weeping.

"We came with a message." Ellyn said, when they finally disentangled themselves from Joshua's grip.

He looked at the two expectantly.

Lapis spoke up. "I had a little notion in my mind. You can tell me if I'm completely wrong, but something tells me you have a small love for Angelina."

Ellyn continued. "We came because we wanted to tell you it's all right if you want to marry Angelina. It won't be hurting us any, and you don't deserve to be alone."

"But how did you know she wasn't married anymore?"

The two exchanged sly looks. "Women's instinct," they both said together, then laughed.

Joshua laughed as well, and he saw Lapis fingering the watch.

"Oh, please don't go yet. I'll never see you again."

"Oh, dear, Joshua. We have our life, and you have yours. So go live your life like you were always meant to."

"And if you and Angelina do marry, we'll be looking down from Heaven with smiles on our faces."

Lapis agreed. Together, she and Ellyn grasped hands. "You ready?" she asked her now dear friend, and Ellyn agreed.

Then they disappeared.

Epilogue

A year later
The wedding ceremony took place a year later. With Joshua finally able to get over his feeling of betrayal, Angelina took a step away from life and looked at it.

What did the rest of her life look like? She didn't want to live alone, but that was the only future she saw.

Until Joshua had popped the question that had rocked her world.

Now her priorities were so different. She had a feeling she'd made the right choice.

As did Joshua. He'd never been happier.

So, the wedding took place, with friends close and abroad gathering for the ceremony.

It was truly a sight to behold.

"Where are we going to go on our honeymoon?" Angelina asked, after the party had calmed down and they had some time to be alone together.

"I don't know. I was thinking we'd go down to Florida, so we could get away from this cold weather."

"That's sounds delightful." Angelina snuggled into his arm.

"We'll get away, and then we'll come back here, and start life anew."

Joshua looked into the horizon. "I like that idea." He looked down at his brand-new wife. "I like that idea a lot."

Not far away, but many years earlier, a small dark-haired woman stood in her backyard, shovel in hand.

She had dug a small hole, and now stared at the watch burning a hole in her hand.

Slowly, carefully, she placed the watch into the deep hole.

Lapis looked at the watch for a moment, then began to put dirt back into the hole. She stared at it, wondering over all the new memories she'd experienced.

Realizing it was probably all a dream, she backed away from the now buried watch and replaced the shovel in the shed.

She heard the sound of her husband's voice, then ran to him.

She jumped into his arms. "I love you." She spoke.

He just smiled at her kindly and repeated her words back.

And they held each other forever.

⁂

AUTHOR'S NOTE

This book served as the sequel to the first edition of What Ever Happened to Ellyn Lyss? If you haven't read that one yet, I urge you to do so. It may explain some things a little better.

Time travel. It's hard because there are so many things, so many inconsistencies that you must watch for.

This short story was fun to write. Imagining that time travel was possible through a magic watch puts things into perspective. What would you do if given access to all the years in the world?

Would you go to the past? Or maybe to the future?

With such incredible power, it was only wise that Lapis buried the watch forever. Harnessing such ability would create an impossible amount of, well, I don't know what.

Because I don't believe in time travel.

And that's the short of it.

The long of it is that everything here happens for a reason. God gave us free will, the ability to make our own choices, despite the consequences.

Everyone's made mistakes. The key is to forgive those errors and move on.

Is that easy?

No.

But you can't travel back in time and fix things you never wished would have happened.

What was the moral of this miniature anecdote?

I don't know. Why are you asking me? I just wanted to write about time travel.

No, but in all seriousness, we need to move on from our mistakes. Joshua had PTSD, because of his childhood and his adult life.

We can't let the past determine our future. We must move on.

We can remember the past, but don't allow it to control or dominate our lives. I guess that's my message. And I hope it's an effective one.

Best wishes,

L. R. Watkins

About the Author

L.R. Watkins loves to write. She currently lives in South Carolina with her parents, her fifteen-year-old twin brother, Brayden, and her three cats. In her free time, she enjoys going on long walks, reading books, and writing, of course. She also likes studying for tests, which she has an uncanny affection for.